"Look." Sarah's whisper was laced with panic. One of the men blocked their exit.

Sarah dashed down another hallway. John followed close behind as the sound of the men's shoes clumping on the floor seemed to get closer.

Around the corner, a door loomed. Sarah grabbed for the handle. "Out?"

"Yes. Go!"

Outside, he followed Sarah around the closest corner and to the back of a brick building.

"There." He pointed across the lot. "Behind the evergreens."

They ducked behind the trees. A small break afforded a protected view of a portion of the parking lot. John leaned forward. Through the needles, he watched a car cruise by. Their pursuers scanned both sides of the parking lot, but as far as John could tell, they didn't have any idea where he and Sarah had gone.

Sarah was trembling, and he took her hand to steady her as he motioned for her to get down. But just as he lowered himself to his knees next to her, the vehicle stopped directly in front of their hiding place.

By sixth grade, **Meghan Carver** knew she wanted to write. After a degree in English from Millikin University, she detoured to law school, completing a Juris Doctorate from Indiana University. She then worked in immigration law and taught college-level composition. Now she homeschools her six children with her husband. When she isn't writing, homeschooling or planning another travel adventure, she is active in her church, sews and reads.

Books by Meghan Carver

Love Inspired Suspense

Under Duress
Deadly Disclosure
Amish Country Amnesia

AMISH COUNTRY AMNESIA

MEGHAN CARVER

H **HARLEQUIN**® LOVE INSPIRED® SUSPENSE

Recycling programs for this product may not exist in your area.

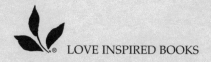

LOVE INSPIRED BOOKS

ISBN-13: 978-1-335-54399-8

Amish Country Amnesia

www.Harlequin.com

Printed in U.S.A.

So teach us to number our days,
that we may apply our hearts unto wisdom.
—*Psalms* 90:12

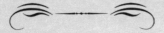

To readers of Amish fiction and stories that explore the miracle of faith, and to readers of suspense and stories that keep you up at night with a chill up your spine. I pray you find this a compelling blend of both.

ONE

Jedediah Miller jerked to the left on the snowmobile, barely skittering it around a stand of barren trees and praying for a fork in the trail up ahead. His hands slipped inside his gloves, and he hitched up his grip on the handlebars. Those two men were following too closely for safety or common courtesy.

On the other side of the trees, his two pursuers edged closer. Jed's heart thumped stronger under his snowmobile suit, and he leaned into the machine, urging it to go faster. A small hill quickly approached, and he flew over it, the skis losing contact with the ground for a moment. As he crashed back down, adrenaline beat through him, his pulse speeding to the thrum of the snowmobile.

The rev of the snowmobiles behind him pushed him on, to a speed that he was sure was not intended for the trail. A speed he wasn't sure he could manage much longer.

These guys drove like professionals, but he was only a casual snowmobiler, saving it for his time off. Trees zipped past him on both sides, and he would have admired the quiet stillness, the hushed beauty of a winter in northern Indiana, the gentle snow-covered hills and the barren trees reaching for every bit of sunshine possible in the muted sky, if not for the two jackals behind him and their mad race.

A *crack* pierced through his concentration, and by instinct, he ducked down on the seat.

They were shooting at him now.

Bark flew off a tree as he whizzed past, a few bits bouncing off his windshield. Apparently, these two weren't good shots, at least when they were going at an outrageous speed on snowmobiles. Judging from the closeness of that tree trunk, though, Jed was sure they could hit their mark when they were at a standstill. Determination to survive drove him on.

He ventured a quick look behind him. Was it Jimmy the Bruise on one of the snowmobiles? His two pursuers were wearing all the protective gear, including helmets and tinted goggles and snowmobile suits completely zipped up. Not an inch of skin or anything identifying was showing, not even Jimmy's telltale purple-and-blue birthmark. All of their gear was black, as well, a rather standard color for snowmobilers. That bit of information wouldn't help at all.

A shiver ran down his arms at the thought of the man at the head of the counterfeiting ring. A nasty birthmark wound its way around the man's neck and down his arm. Being on the police force had brought Jed into contact with a lot of different people, but there was no getting used to a guy who looked like that. No matter how long he lived, Jed would never forget the look of that dark splotch that appeared to hold the man's throat in a vice grip.

Jed had seen that mark plenty of times in the past twelve months of undercover work that had taken him from Fort Wayne to Indianapolis to Cincinnati and back to Fort Wayne. It had been a harrowing experience that still haunted his dreams, both in the daytime and at night, but it was going to pay off. In just a few weeks, his testimony in court would put the counterfeiters behind bars, at least most of them. Jimmy the Bruise and another had gone missing, escaped from police custody.

A third shot pinged off the back of his snowmobile. The case would fall apart without Jed's testimony. If they could kill him, the counterfeiting ring would get off easy and be back in business within months. Only Jed could put them away for good.

It was time to lose these two yahoos. Without backup available, he couldn't apprehend them. He wanted to kick himself for forgetting his phone that morning. But at least he could try to save himself and the valuable testimony he possessed. Then he would call for a search of the area. There were only so many places to hide in and around the heavily Amish community of Nappanee, and he couldn't imagine that any Amish would shelter two people as prone to violence as these were. Jed tossed up a prayer for the safety of any of the peace-loving Amish who might come into contact with these two thugs.

He inhaled as deeply as he could with the restrictions of his helmet. Fresh oxygen infused him as he leaned his body weight forward on the snowmobile to increase the speed. What was supposed to have been a restful week off in the stillness of northern Indiana had suddenly morphed into a deadly chase. Jed allowed a brief thought of what his life might be like without the danger or violence of being a police officer, but the snowmobile shot up another ridge and brought him back to the present.

A small pocket of evergreens stood ahead, to the side of the trail. At the last moment, just at the edge of the grove, he leaned left and gripped the handlebars, shooting behind the trees and off the trail. The snow wasn't as packed here, but he increased the throttle, urging the machine to go faster. He wound through the trees, dodging boulders, but the two men continued behind him. At least the shooting had stopped, but that was probably just because they needed both hands on the handlebars to stay in a forward motion.

He searched his memories of the area frantically. Where could he hide? It had been years since he'd been here. And he was limited in where he could go because of the snowmobile. Plowed roads were definitely not conducive to a vehicle that ran on skis. So, he couldn't lead them to a sheriff's office, and he certainly didn't want to take that violence where there might be people.

A small stream burbled to his right, large rocks and snow-covered foliage on either side, and he leaned left to steer the snowmobile away from the water. Even though the sound of their engines told him they were fast approaching, he dared another glance back. They were too close. Much too close for safety.

He faced forward again as the machine arced to the left. A tree rushed up in front of him, and he jerked the snowmobile to the right. But another tree rose up in that direction. He pushed his body to the side to steer the machine away, but it was too late. The fiberglass front of the snowmobile crumpled into the solid trunk of the tree, killing the engine. Jed couldn't control his body, and like a rag doll, he pitched forward. His helmet hit the windshield, and his head slammed against the inside of the helmet.

Pain shot through his frontal lobe. Lightning seemed to flash behind his eyes. Lifted from the seat by the impact, he soared forward and to the right. The limbs of the tree and the snow-covered underbrush flew by. He landed in the bushes on his back, snow falling on him and brambles tearing at his nylon suit. Pain coursed through his body as he rolled over just in time to see his snowmobile burst into flames.

He jerked off his goggles and helmet and gasped for air as the cold bit at his skin. Despite the snow that had fallen on him, he was still exposed in his gray snowmobiling suit. Surreptitiously, moving only his eyes, he looked toward the boulders at the edge of the stream. He would be better camouflaged among those rocks.

His two pursuers had finally stopped, but just a few yards from his wreck. Jed couldn't see their eyes through their goggles, but from the tilt of their helmets, he surmised they were watching the fire.

In an army crawl, lifted up only on his elbows, Jed inched toward the rocks around the stream. Aches ricocheted through every inch of his body. The closest boulder seemed miles away, moving at that speed, but it was his only hope.

Suddenly, one of the men turned, appearing to survey the area. Jed buried his face in the snow and froze. There was something about a face and, in particular, eyes that always seemed to draw attention, and Jed determined that he would not be found out simply because he couldn't look away. He waited for what seemed like an eternity, praying for safety and courage and survival, his muscles taut. When nothing happened, he slowly lifted his head, just enough to be able to scan the area.

The men still sat on their snowmobiles, watching as Jed's machine burned. If there was anything Jed had learned in twelve months of undercover work, it was patience.

He could wait there, lying in the snow, as long as necessary.

After a few minutes, the men turned around to look behind them. Jed grabbed his opportunity.

Still lying nearly prostrate, he scuttled toward the rocks and catapulted himself over the closest grouping of boulders. He landed on his back on an unyielding surface, and a sharp rock caught the side of his head on the way down. A fire of pain shot through his skull, and he reached up a hand to touch a warm, sticky spot. The sky swirled and danced unnaturally above him until all went black.

Sarah Burkholder stood at the kitchen sink, her hands immersed in the warm soapy water, and stared out the window at the snow-covered barn. An apple pie rested on the counter, its aroma of cinnamon and nutmeg filling the roomy kitchen. The pie would be a welcome addition to supper.

The mechanical whine of a snowmobile had not been far off that afternoon, the noise an unwelcome intrusion into her normally peaceful world. Her home was miles from the snowmobile trail through the state park, but it sounded as if a rider had left the beaten path. She would be glad when he stopped his racing and returned to the park.

An envelope propped on the windowsill drew her attention. Her mother's careful handwriting scrawled Sarah's name and address across the front. Sarah had read it so many times that she almost had it memorized. In no uncertain terms, her mother had urged her to return to live with them in Lancaster County. She had written that they could sell at the market together, and Sarah would be supported and encouraged by the love of her family. Her real point in writing, it seemed, was to tell her of one particular widower who had been asking after her.

Sarah rubbed the back of her hand across her chin. She remembered the man her mother had mentioned in her letter. He was nice-looking enough, and kind. But there never had been a spark between them. Still though, would it be better than being alone? Did *Gott* only grant one love in a lifetime?

The fresh dilemma swirled in her mind. Should she continue to teach school in the Indiana Amish community she had grown to love? Or should she return to Lancaster County, to Pennsylvania and the family she had left behind? A tear escaped and trickled down her cheek at the memory of her husband. Life had changed drastically in that one terrible moment, and not for the better.

Even though she had committed to teaching for the entire school year and did not need to decide for a while, she promised herself she would pray during the winter break and seek the will of *Gott* for her future.

She dried her hands on a nearby towel and then dabbed the corner of her apron to her eyes.

How could it have been *Gott*'s will that her husband die in that buggy accident? That was best for her? For their daughter, Lyddie?

Ach. That was not the Amish way, to question the authority of *Gott.* Another tear overflowed, and she lifted the apron again. *Father, if Thou be willing, remove this cup from me. Nevertheless, not my will, but Thine, be done.* At least she had Lyddie, the joy of her life, although the poor child was growing up without her *daed* and at only six years old.

Where was Lyddie anyway? She had been instructed to stay close to the house and barn today.

Sarah retrieved her heavy winter cape and bonnet from the hook near the door and stepped out onto the back porch. The noise of other snowmobiles was a little louder outside, but then they moved away. She inhaled deeply, the winter air slicing through her lungs, and savored the return of the stillness.

But she still needed to find Lyddie. With snowmobiles around, the child ought to stay closer to home. Most of their *Englisch* neighbors were mindful of those in the Amish community, but Lyddie still had chores to complete, as well. The floor needed to be swept and the eggs gathered.

She walked to the end of the porch, her gaze sweeping from the barn to the tree line. "Lyddie!" But there was no telling if she was in earshot.

Sarah stepped back inside and changed quickly into her heavy snow boots. She would have to go searching on foot.

As Sarah pulled the door closed behind her, the child broke from the trees, followed closely by Snowball, their brown-and-white malamute. A look of alarm held fast on her face as she ran as best she could through the snow, a few blond curls that had struggled free from her *kapp* flying behind her. "*Mamm*! A man. An *Englischer*! He is hurt. He has been attacked." Lyddie gasped for breath as she skidded to a stop in front of her mother. The dog barked as if to urge Sarah to help, then turned and faced back toward the woods.

Sarah's hand flew to cover her mouth and then migrated south to cover her heart as if it could still the wild beat at Lyddie's news. An attack? She prayed the child was mistaken.

Lyddie pulled at her mother's hand. "*Mamm.* We must help the man."

"*Jah.* We must." She paused. "In case it is needed, hitch the sled to Snowball."

Lyddie ran to the barn to retrieve the sled she had rigged to hitch to the large snow dog. Sarah stepped back inside to grab a quilt, and when she returned to the porch, daughter and dog were ready to go. With no idea what she might find, she at least wanted another way to supply warmth.

Sarah pulled her cape about her and stepped out to follow her daughter. "Show me where he is."

She followed as Lyddie led Snowball and retraced her tracks in the snow, babbling like the brook in springtime about hiding in the trees as the snowmobiles came closer and watching two snowmobiles chase another snowmobile and the man who then did not move. The dog bounded alongside, strangely quiet, as if she knew her barking could draw unwanted attention. After hiking for several minutes, Sarah felt the acrid odor of smoke fill her nostrils.

She pushed Lyddie faster, clumping behind in her snow boots, as they followed the sight of a thin plume of gray smoke rising from over another hill. *Gott, have mercy.*

They crested the hill, and Lyddie led her through some trees and into a tiny clearing next to the creek. Sarah knew it well. Some wild raspberry bushes grew not far away where they would pick berries in the heat come August. But now, everything was covered with the white blanket of winter even as more snow fell.

At the site, Sarah gasped. *How could anyone have survived that?* A red-and-black snowmobile had crashed into a tree, and flames rose from its crumpled form. She rushed forward, the heat warming her face. Instinctively, she held out an arm to hold Lyddie back from the fire.

She turned toward her daughter, not taking her eyes from the wreckage. "Lyddie, where is the *Englischer*? Show me."

The girl moved past Sarah's arm and skirted around the flames. She held out a hand to Snowball and he sat, then she headed for some boulders at the edge of the creek bed. "Here. He has not moved."

Sarah surveyed the area. With what Lyddie had said about the man being attacked, she didn't want to risk any danger on their part. But all seemed still and silent there in the woods.

On the other side of the boulders, a man in a gray snowmobile suit lay with a fine layer of snow on him. A gash on the side of his head trickled a bright red flow of blood. A little bit of blood had dripped onto his shoulder and the rock where he had apparently hit his head. His snowmobile suit was torn in a couple of places, but other than that, he appeared well. His eyes were closed as if in sleep, but Sarah flew to his side. She kneeled on the snow next to him and pulled down the collar of his protective jacket to feel for a pulse. His heartbeat was strong. She released a breath she hadn't been aware she was holding. The man was still alive. She lowered her head and turned to listen for his breath. It was even and steady. She then gently felt every bone, but each felt solid and unharmed.

So far, everything had checked normal, but he still had not reacted to her touch.

She prodded his shoulder, lifted his hand, rolled his ankle. "Hello? Can you hear me? Can you wake up?"

He remained unresponsive.

A chill shook through her. Whether it was fear or the cold did not matter. She needed to be careful of her surroundings, for her sake, for the sake of her daughter and for the sake of this unknown man. But she also needed to get him to warmth and shelter to treat his wounds.

She shook her head, a desperate attempt to understand human beings. What kind of person would allow an injured man to lie in the snow and not care for him? Obviously, not a good one. Lyddie had said that there were two on snowmobiles chasing the man. She had even mentioned a gun in the hand of one of the pursuers. Had they hoped to kill him? Thought he was dead?

Sarah stood and looked back to the site of the accident and what was left of the tracks in the snow. Thankfully, all remained quiet. But what if the attackers returned? Lyddie had said they had driven off and out of sight. But if they were evil enough to leave a hurt man here, a man who appeared to be dead, what would they do to an innocent Amish woman and her daughter? There were no other footprints besides their own and a couple of sets of prints near where the snowmobiles had stopped. It seemed as if they had dismounted but then left again. There were also no other snowmobile tracks, but the falling snow was quickly filling in everything.

Soon, there would be no visible signs of any human presence left.

The best thing to do would be to get the man to the house immediately. To safety. A neighbor had a telephone in his barn for business, but the neighbor was farther from here than the distance to her own home. If his pursuers did return, Sarah did not want to be there, exposed, nor did she want the injured man to be, whoever he was.

"Lyddie." Sarah kept her voice to a loud whisper. "Bring the sled. There." She pointed to a path around the rocks.

As the dog brought the sled, Sarah leaned down to the man. "My name is Sarah, and my daughter, Lyddie, is here." Could he hear her? She had no way to know, but she needed to try. "You are injured, and I am taking you to my house. We will load you on the sled."

Lyddie led Snowball to pull the sled until it sat alongside the man. Squatting down, Sarah put her arms under the man's shoulders and instructed Lyddie to get him by the ankles. "We will move you now," she said to the man, then nodded to Lyddie, and together they swung him onto the sled, then tucked the quilt about him.

The man moved his head from one side to

the other, a low groan issuing from his lips, but his eyes did not open.

With Lyddie's encouragement, the dog strained against the harness to haul the sled. Sarah grabbed the handle and helped to pull through the snow, as well. As the hum of snowmobiles sounded again in the distance, Sarah urged the dog to haul faster. Safety behind her locked doors was close, and her hands perspired within her gloves at the thought of being out in the woods if those men returned.

The man continued a low groan off and on through most of the walk back to the house. At the back door, Sarah released Snowball and rubbed her ears, conveying her gratitude for the dog's help. The stranger had moved in the sled, so Sarah leaned down and shook his shoulder again. "Can you hear me? We are home, and I need you to stand and walk inside. Can you get up?"

When he didn't stand, Sarah grasped one arm and put Lyddie on the other. Together, they pulled him to a sitting position. That movement seemed to awaken something inside him, for he stood, leaning heavily on them. With his eyes mostly closed, he staggered into the house as Sarah guided him into the downstairs guest bedroom. He was not overly tall, but his solid form filled out his snowmobile suit, and Sarah knew she would never be able to get him up the stairs.

As he lay down on the quilt, his head thrashed and his eyelids fluttered as if with some internal struggle. His eyes opened suddenly, and she gasped to look into such vivid green eyes. He startled, grabbing toward his hip as if reaching for something, a harsh and intense look on his face.

She jumped back, clutching her skirt.

Perhaps he was the dangerous one after all?

TWO

An eerie quiet filtered through his mind, a stillness that felt foreign and uncomfortable. With what felt like great effort, he opened his eyes only to find more darkness, softened slightly by moonlight coming through a window. Before he could form a coherent thought or try to lift his head, the darkness consumed him again.

His next sensation was a sharpness in his temple. Without even opening his eyes, he knew it was daylight. He released his eyelids to a slit. Bright sunshine streamed through windows on either side of the bed.

He lifted a hand to his forehead, trying to locate the source of the stabbing pain. His hand came into contact with what felt like a bandage, but the hurt seemed to come from all over his head. Just the act of moving his arm made him aware of an aching soreness that consumed his entire body. Shading his eyes, he opened them further.

The walls around him were a stark white. Light blue curtains hung at the windows, but they were thin enough that they did not block the light very much. He was in a bed, covered with a colorful quilt, a wood armoire standing against the wall across from him. Near the door, a young girl with a blue dress and white cap on her head sat in a straight-backed chair, reading a book. She must have noticed his movement, for she looked up and their stares locked. Her mouth formed a perfect O of surprise, and she dashed from the room.

Before he could try to sit up, the girl returned with a young woman who wore a similar dress and cap.

The woman pressed her lips together as if concerned, and tiny crinkling lines formed around her eyes. But her gaze radiated warmth and care. "How are you?" Her voice was quiet and calming.

She pulled the chair up to the bedside and sat, her hands clasped in her lap. Her face seemed to be completely devoid of makeup, and yet a beauty radiated from her that he hadn't seen in… Well, he couldn't remember when.

He cleared his throat, trying to summon

his voice. His mind was a complete blank, yet a sense of discomfort, danger even, seemed to hover over him. How was he? "I'm… I'm sore."

"I am glad to see you are awake. I bandaged the cut on your forehead last night." She fluttered her hand up to the side of his head. "May I check it?"

He nodded. She peeled back part of the bandage, her touch a whisper against his skin. "It has stopped bleeding. That is *gut*." She stood and stepped to the window, lifting the curtain to look out. She stood there a moment, surveying, a frown creasing her brow. But as she returned to the chair, she seemed to force a small smile. "Now. Introductions. I am Sarah Burkholder. This is my house. And this," she motioned the girl forward, "is my daughter, Lyddie."

She looked at him, expectation etched around her eyes and mouth.

But his mind was blank, a black hole of nothingness. He closed his eyes to block out any distractions, including the woman's pretty face and the sweetness of the little girl, and searched for any information about who he was. What was his name? What was his job? What had happened yesterday that landed him here in this home? And why did he have such a pervasive feeling of danger?

He had no idea.

He opened his eyes to find the woman still watching him, waiting for an answer. "I don't know."

Confusion flitted across her face. "You do not know your own name?"

He thought again. "No."

"Where do you live?"

Again, he searched and came up blank. "I don't know. Here? With you?"

"No. Not here." She giggled, a musical sound that calmed him. "What is your job?"

"I don't know. What can you tell me about yourself? Where is your husband? Where are we? How did you get me here?"

She held out a hand. "In good time. First, I will send Lyddie to fetch the doctor."

At a nod from her mother, the girl ran out of the room. A few moments later, an exterior door slammed.

The woman settled herself again on the chair. "My husband was killed two years ago when a car hit his buggy. We are near Nappanee in Indiana, in the home my husband built when we moved here. We are Amish." She gestured to her dark blue dress, her white apron, her starched *kapp*.

"Yes." Somehow, he knew the word *Amish* and had a vague inkling of what it meant. That's why the girl went running for the doctor. There would be no telephone in the house.

"Lyddie and I brought you here on a sled pulled by our malamute, Snowball. I did not see it, but she told me that you were chased by two men on snowmobiles. You crashed into a tree. I think you hit your head on a rock by the creek."

"What about the two men?"

"They left you. They must have thought you were dead." She paused, clearly thinking through her next words. When she spoke again, it was haltingly. "I do not like to bother the sheriff. He is…not friendly to me. To our way of life. But I will contact him if you wish."

"No!" He struggled to sit up in bed, ache consuming his body. Where did that vehemence come from? A dark foreboding invaded his mind when he thought of law enforcement, and he clutched his head in an effort to calm himself. "I… I can't explain it. I don't know why. But no, don't bring the police into this. Not yet." Maybe if his memories returned and he could figure out who he was and what sort of situation he was in, then he could involve law enforcement. "I wouldn't know what to tell them anyway."

She laid a hand on the quilt as if to calm him. "I will respect your wishes. But you need a name. Are you sure you cannot remember your own?"

"My head aches so terribly that it hurts to try to remember anything."

"May I call you John?" She tilted her head, and one side of her mouth quirked up. "John is a good Bible name meaning *Yahweh is gracious*. Would you not agree that the Lord has been gracious to you, saving you from worse harm?"

Something pinged in his brain. "Yes, the Lord has been gracious."

"You are a religious man? You believe?"

A comfortable warmth filled him as she asked the questions. "I don't know for sure, but I think I do."

"That is *gut*. But also, you are a *John Doe*. Is that not what the *Englisch* call a person with no name?"

"How do you know that?" This beautiful Amish woman whose presence soothed him was certainly a mystery.

She ducked her head, the top of her *kapp* catching the sunlight. "I love to read."

As if to change the subject, she stood and crossed the room to the armoire, pulling out an Amish-looking pair of trousers and shirt as well as a pair of suspenders. "Your clothes need to be laundered. You may put these on for the time being. They belong to my brother, but he left them here after his last visit."

A whistle sounded from another room, and she laid the clothes at the foot of the bed.

"That is the kettle. I will bring you some herbal tea. Chamomile. It will help relieve your headache and your muscle soreness. Do you like tea?" She stood and moved to the door.

Did he like tea? He had no idea, but the lovely Sarah was so kind and so accommodating that he would drink just about anything she could bring him. A nod would have to suffice to show his agreement, as a spasm of pain shot through his head.

Why couldn't he remember anything? Who was he? Why was he there, in the Amish countryside, and who were the two men from yesterday? A blankness settled over him, but it was cloaked in darkness as the overwhelming sensation of danger returned, and he feared not only for his future but also for the future of the beautiful widow who sheltered him.

* * *

Sarah dropped the bag of tea leaves into the cup and slowly poured the boiling water over it. She inhaled deeply of the soothing scent, in need of some calming herself after the events of the prior twenty-four hours.

A shiver threatened her, and she returned the kettle to the propane-powered stove top before she stepped to the window to survey the yard again. Her sleep had been fitful the night before, her dreams filled with burning snowmobiles and strange men come to harm her and her daughter.

Who was this man in her spare bedroom, and what sort of danger had he brought to her peaceful household?

For what must have been at least the tenth time, she mentally retraced the events of yesterday. It certainly had looked from the snowmobile tracks like this man in her house was the one being chased. But did it follow, then, that he was innocent? Good? She had no way of knowing, and it seemed, neither did he. Did it matter? She had a Christian obligation to help those in need.

As she watched, the doctor's car pulled into her drive. Lyddie flew out of the passenger side and toward the kitchen door. *Ach,* the child would be so excited about a ride in the car she would chatter of nothing else for days. The tall, thin Dr. Jones unfolded himself from the driver's seat, retrieved his black bag from the back seat and approached the door as Lyddie waited for him. The hair around his temples sported more gray than the last time Sarah had seen him, and a pair of glasses perched on his pointed nose.

He stepped inside the back room, and Sarah rushed to hang up his coat. "Dr. Jones, *danki* for coming."

"Hello, Sarah. I'm always glad to visit my Amish friends and keep up the traditions of my father. Family and community are important to some of us Englishers, as well." A teasing twinkle sparkled in his eye. He looked pointedly at the remains of the apple pie on the stove top.

"Would you like a piece of pie before you go? I would not want you to leave hungry." The banter was as old a tradition as the house calls, but Sarah relished her friendship with the doctor.

"If you insist." He smiled with warmth and touched her shoulder before he turned toward the downstairs bedroom. "Now, Lyddie tells me you have a man in there who was in a snowmobiling accident yesterday?"

Sarah filled him in on the details she knew,

few as they were, including the man's apparent amnesia, as she led him into the room and pointed him to the chair at the bedside. John had changed into the Amish clothing, creating quite a change in his appearance, and was resting on top of the quilt.

"Dr. Jones, this is John. At least, he has agreed to be called by that name. I gave him my brother's clothes to put on." She turned to the patient. "John, this is Dr. Jones."

John attempted a smile, although it looked painful, and shook hands with the doctor. "You make house calls? I didn't know anyone did that anymore."

Dr. Jones laid his black bag on the bed next to John and opened it. "My father made house calls, so I choose to continue that practice, at least with the Amish. They have a bit more difficulty in getting to the office than other folks. And there's never a poor return on being neighborly."

As the doctor retrieved his stethoscope from his bag and instructed John to unbutton his shirt, Sarah stepped out to finish making the tea and shooed Lyddie upstairs to her room to work on her stitching. She took as long as she could and then grasped the tray and stepped toward the door. "May I come in?"

"Yes, that's fine."

She entered the room to find the doctor slowly moving an instrument back and forth in front of John. He followed it with his eyes but without moving his head. But when he spotted her, her breath hitched as his green eyes smiled at her.

The doctor placed the instrument back in his bag and snapped it shut. He stood and moved back to allow Sarah to place the tray on the bedside table. "Your patient seems quite well, Sarah. You bandaged that nasty cut on his head quite admirably, and it should heal nicely. Apart from that, a little soreness and his memory loss, I would say he is in fine shape. I don't see any problems."

"That is *gut*."

He held up his hands in caution. "However, my ability to examine him is limited here. I would suggest that as soon as he feels able, he get to the hospital for an MRI and a thorough examination." He pulled a small bottle from his bag and placed it on the table. "Here is some acetaminophen, in case your chamomile tea doesn't relieve the pain like he wants. However," the doctor turned to John, "you should take it only as a last resort. Allergies to acetaminophen are rare, but because you can't remember your medical history or what medicine you might be allergic to, we don't know how this might affect you."

"What about my memory, Doctor?"

"Well, amnesia is a tricky thing, and we medical professionals still don't know much about it. Your memory will most likely return in time. How long I cannot say."

John shook the doctor's hand and thanked him for coming, then accepted the cup of tea from Sarah.

Dr. Jones looked at Sarah and nodded toward the kitchen, and she stepped in front to lead him there. As she approached the pie, he laid a hand on her arm. "Can you wrap it to go, please? I have an appointment and can't stay."

"*Jah*, if you wish."

As she packaged two slices of the apple pie, he stood close enough that he could keep his voice low. "I admire you for taking this stranger in and caring for him. But I want to warn you, as well. I know you have, at least, a rifle for hunting. You should keep that close for protection for you and Lyddie. Just in case. If you don't need protection from this stranger, then you might need protection from whoever caused the accident yesterday."

She handed the pie to him. "*Danki*, doctor, but you know that is not the Amish way. I will trust *Gott* for His protection and His guidance."

Dr. Jones grasped his bag in one hand and the pie in the other, and Sarah moved to open the door for him. "I knew that would be your answer, but I felt the need to say it." He paused, then looked her in the eye. "One more thing. I think I see a bit of resemblance between John and Mary Miller. There's something about his eyes that makes me think of her."

"*Mammi* Mary? The widow who lives over on Woodbridge Road?"

"Yes, but maybe it's nothing." He stepped outside. "I'll pray for you and for the stranger, and don't hesitate to contact me if you need help."

Sarah closed the door gently behind him and then turned the lock until it thudded into place. The rifle? It still rested in its place on top of the cabinets. She kept it cleaned and in good working order, but it had not been used since before her husband was killed.

No, there it would stay. She would trust *Gott* and His protection.

But a wiggle of worry wormed itself down her back. Who was this strange man? Had he brought danger with him? Had she willingly brought into her house a wolf that she had dressed in Amish clothing?

THREE

John helped as best he could in cleaning up their simple breakfast of sticky rolls and scrambled eggs, but his skills were so lacking that he figured he hadn't done much kitchen work before. His shoulders sagged at the thought of how long it might take to regain his memory.

Sarah was jittery as she quickly washed the dishes and laid them out on a towel to dry. Between keeping an eye on him and jumping up to look out the window, she barely sat for the meal. He hoped his presence wasn't too upsetting to her, but how could it not be? She didn't know him, and yet here he sat, completely dependent upon her goodness. What kind of man was he? Could he be trusted? Was he honorable? Neither of them knew.

As she laid the last glass on the drying towel, he ventured a suggestion. "I think we need to head back to the scene of the accident. Or was it an attack? It's frustrating not even to know what happened yesterday." He rubbed a hand over the knot in the back of his neck and took a deep breath. "If I could just remember—something, anything—I might know what to do next. But there could be something at the site to help me remember. Fill in some of the emptiness. It's a good time to look because of the bright sunshine. If there's any clue there, we should be able to find it."

Lyddie ran for her heavy cape. "*Mamm*, may I take Snowball and the sled?"

Sarah turned from the sink to her daughter, her eyes wide. "It has not yet been decided." She set her worried look on John. "Do you think it is safe?"

What *did* he think? With this amnesia, his mind felt like it couldn't think, or at least it was difficult to think. "You said there was no one there when you found me. And obviously, no one has found us here. To be completely honest, I don't know. But it seems that it should be, and I don't have any other ideas for how to figure out who I am or where I'm supposed to be. I think this is my only chance."

"*Jah*. I think you are right." She hung up the towel and headed for the stairs. "I will put on an extra pair of leggings for warmth, and we shall go. Lyddie, same for you. And we will take Snowball but not the sled. John, what do you think?"

"Yes, the sled could get in the way, but the dog could be helpful in staying alert."

A few minutes later, John had bundled on a heavy wool coat and hat that Sarah had in the barn, and they set off toward the site of his snowmobile crash. The sunshine made the snow sparkle, but it did not add any warmth to the day, and he pulled the coat closer around him. Snowball frisked about, her white tail curled up over her back. John had no doubt that the dog would sniff out danger before he saw it. But John still couldn't help constantly scanning their surroundings for anything remotely suspicious.

As he crested the top of the ridge, John got his first good look at the snowmobile. But all that remained were charred parts and crumpled fiberglass. A whisper of smoke halfheartedly rose from the wreckage, but it was not enough to mark their location to anyone nearby. He held out an arm to stop Sarah and Lyddie. He listened for a full minute, but the only sound close by was the panting of the malamute.

He skidded down the slope and stopped

next to the debris. Would it summon up any memories? The vinyl seat remained intact, and he tried to picture himself sitting on it, his hands on the handlebars. His snowmobile suit was gray. He knew that because he had seen it. But nothing dislodged any memories.

"Spread out a bit," he instructed Sarah and Lyddie. "Look for anything that might be the least bit helpful."

Sarah circled around the creek bed, where she had found him the day before, her head bent to the task. Lyddie followed behind her mother, overturning a few rocks. She wandered toward the woods, picking up sticks and throwing them into the trees, and then returned toward John. Her full blue skirt swished against her black snow boots, and snow that had fallen from the trees rested on her shoulders and *kapp*. Snowball followed her faithfully, sniffing in her footsteps.

The child was adorable, but John forced himself to return his gaze to the remains of the accident site.

"Look! I found something!" Lyddie's squeal of delight drew him quickly to her side. She bent to the ground and retrieved from the snow a piece of metal that reflected the bright sunshine.

The snow quickly brushed off of the edges,

and she handed it to John. "What is it? What does it say?"

Sarah appeared at his side, her breath puffing in small clouds. "It is the badge of a police officer."

"Fort Wayne Police Department," John read. "Is that far from here?"

"It is over an hour by car." She shrugged. "We pay a driver and go to shop sometimes. Is this yours?"

"I don't know. It could be mine. Or it could belong to one of the men who Lyddie says attacked me. Let's keep looking. Maybe there's some identification."

As Sarah and Lyddie pushed snow away from the debris, questions pinged in John's mind. Could the badge be his, thrown off him in the wreck? What about a weapon? Was he a police officer?

Ten minutes of thorough searching yielded nothing more.

John examined the badge in his hand, trying to force himself to remember. "So, I could be a police officer. Or maybe I'm not. There's no way to know if this badge belongs to me because there's no name on it, just a number, and I don't remember any numbers. I suppose it could have been thrown off me in the wreck, but if I am a law-enforcement officer, then where is my weapon?" He pulled off a glove and rubbed his temple. A dull throb began to echo through his head. *Or am I the criminal the police were chasing?*

"This does not help with any memories?" Sarah gazed at him with eyes crinkled and warm with tenderness and compassion.

Before he could answer, Snowball perked up her ears and uttered a low growl.

Lyddie dropped to the snow next to her, a mittened hand on her back. "What is it, Snowball?"

"Shh." John held out his hand to silence them. He listened intently, straining against the growing thrum of the headache. A machine was approaching. A snowmobile?

"Could it be someone to help?" Sarah kept her voice to a whisper.

John shook his head. "No way to know. But we need to get out of here. I can't explain why, but I don't want us here when the snowmobile arrives." He nodded toward the woods. "Into the trees. Quickly."

He grasped Sarah's hand to lead her, and he was instantly warmed by her touch. Sarah threw him a startled look but did not draw away. She urged Lyddie toward the woods and called for Snowball to follow.

Several feet into the tree line, John made

sure Sarah was tucked behind a large cottonwood. He looked back toward the clearing just in time to see a snowmobile emerge from the far side. A glance back to Sarah revealed that she had grabbed hold of Snowball's collar. Lyddie stood on the other side of the dog, her hand resting on the dog's head as if to keep her calm.

It would have to do for now. Their movement through the trees, to head for Sarah's house, would only draw attention to them. And since they could never outrun a snowmobile, it was best to hide.

John crouched behind another tree and turned his attention to the approaching snowmobile.

The driver pulled up to within a few feet of the crash debris. He killed the engine and then dismounted. He wore a typical snowmobile suit, black with white trim, and he appeared to be a thick man underneath. But since the man wore a helmet and goggles, John could not tell anything more about him.

The man surveyed the accident site, then picked up a stick and poked at the debris. When he seemed satisfied, he dropped the stick and slowly scanned the surrounding area.

Snowball continued to pant, although the

sound was so quiet that John had to strain to hear it. Lyddie put her hand over her mouth and clamped it shut. John wanted to tell her that the dog would not take kindly to that, but he didn't dare whisper or leave his hiding place. The dog pulled her head away, a low whine issuing forth as she shook her muzzle free.

John dared a peek around his tree. The man had taken a couple of steps in their direction. He had removed his gloves and tucked them in a cargo pocket and was working on his goggles and helmet. John's gut clenched at the possibility of being discovered, but all he could do was wait.

With his head cocked, the snowmobile driver stared at the trees, a look of deep concentration on his face as if he were listening. Had he heard Snowball whine? It could have sounded like a wild animal, and yet there weren't many animals out in the winter. John turned back to Sarah and Lyddie just in time to see Sarah move to correct the girl, probably for holding the dog's mouth shut.

As she reached out a hand, Sarah seemed to lose her balance, and she wobbled out from her hiding place.

Helpless where he was, John watched the man's stare zero in on Sarah as she leaned out. She immediately grasped the trunk of the tree and pulled herself behind it, but not before a loud inhalation escaped.

John's heart beat wildly against his rib cage, and he swallowed down bile as his stomach churned at the look of evil on the man's face.

Sarah's gasp seemed to echo through the empty woods. She shot her hand up to cover her mouth, but it was too late to stifle the sound.

He had seen her.

Whoever that man was that radiated evil intent, he now knew they were there.

But just as startling was the blue-and-purple bruise mark around the man's neck and on his hand, peeking out from the cuff of his jacket. Even in the midst of her fear, a small wave of sympathy rose for the man with such a birthmark. Her gaze flew to his eyes again, and the sympathy quickly disappeared at the malice she saw there.

She clutched at what felt like safety—the solidness of the tree trunk. Her feet felt mired in the deep snow and the boots. She could not run if she tried.

Lyddie stood from kneeling next to the malamute and looked at Sarah, her eyes wide with questioning and fright. The girl was just trying to be helpful, but it could get them all killed.

Gott, help us!

But in that moment of desperate prayer, Lyddie's whisper filtered in.

"*Mamm*! That is the man! I saw him yesterday!" Even through the mitten, the point of her finger was unmistakable. "See his neck and hand? Scary!"

"Lyddie!" Her whisper came out more harsh than she intended. She needed to have a talk with her daughter about kindness and compassion when others looked different, but now was not the time. "Get back!"

As Sarah grasped Lyddie's shoulder and pulled her behind the tree, she snuck another glance through a few fall leaves that still clung to several branches. The man's eyes were wide, and a small smile snaked across his lips as if he understood the situation. Perspiration dampened her brow despite the cold of the winter day. She struggled to even her breathing and remain calm, but her breath continued to puff out in short spurts.

She looked at John, and he simply held a finger to his lips to indicate she should remain quiet.

At the very least, the man had to know now

that she had been around the site of the crash and, most likely, knew something about John. He knew that she was involved.

If there was any doubt of the man's knowledge of her, it was all erased as he drew a weapon out of a cargo pocket and pointed it at her.

Her breath hitched. She clutched at Lyddie and Snowball, both to protect them and to keep from collapsing.

He slowly approached the tree line, each step an ominous crunch in the hardened snow.

"Sarah." John's whisper filtered through the panicked haze in her mind. She forced her gaze away from the gun to see John motioning for them to run deeper into the woods.

Somehow, she moved her head enough to nod her assent.

With a death grip on the arm of her only child, she turned to run. Her heavy winter boots felt glued to the ground, too bulky to move, but she clunked along for a few steps. The weight of her despair sank her farther down into the ground. How could she possibly outrun a bullet at her slow speed? *Gott* was always there, she reminded herself, and she begged for His protection.

The cracking sound of a gun firing rang in her ears. Would she feel the pain of death?

Or would she just suddenly find herself in the presence of *Gott*? Who would care for Lyddie?

A strong force—a hand—pushed on her back. Strong enough to push her down. She landed face-down in the snow, her hand still on Lyddie, who fell next to her.

Lyddie turned to look at her, fear contorting her face.

"I love you," Sarah mouthed.

Then she closed her eyes, praying that her death would be quick and painless.

FOUR

John kept his hand on Sarah's back, waiting for a second gunshot to ring out through the silence of the snowy woods. Sarah's back hitched and spasmed underneath his touch with her shallow and uneven breathing. The terror she must be feeling, a gun pointed at her and her only child, must far surpass his own fear. He wished he could take it away, but he could only provide a human connection and pray.

The quiet of the winter afternoon echoed around them in between the swooshing of his heartbeat in his eardrums. What must have been only seconds of waiting for death seemed to stretch into eternity.

Where was the gunshot? What was their would-be killer waiting for?

The squeal of car tires broke the silence. John jerked his hand away from Sarah in surprise. They must be close to a road. The sound of a car missing traction on gravel hit his ears, and he turned his head just enough to see the man return to his snowmobile.

Sarah lifted her head out of the snow, the arch of her eyebrows telegraphing the question of their safety to John.

Were they saved? Or was that the man's reinforcement, come to seal their fate?

He nodded *no*, hoping she understood his message not to move.

The man paused to look back at Sarah and Lyddie.

John tucked his head down, fearing that to make eye contact would only further anger his aggressor. A grunt sounded, and the slip of a nylon snowmobile suit in motion slid past John's ears.

Another squeal of tires reverberated through the woods. John snuck another glance behind in time to see the man tuck his weapon into a cargo pocket. The man quickly hopped on his snowmobile, revved it and took off through the trees in the direction of the road.

John let out a breath and forced himself to release the tension in his muscles.

"He has gone, John?" Sarah was still staring at him.

He nodded. "I believe so."

Remaining on her stomach, she scooted to Lyddie, scooping her into her embrace. The two lay together, and John watched her comfort her child, her hand stroking Lyddie's arm and brushing hair away from her face.

Had he had a mother like that? He stretched through his mind for a memory until an ache pinged in his forehead. No images or feelings surfaced. His life remained a void.

He passed a hand over his forehead and retrieved his hat from the snow a couple of feet away. With the danger gone, at least for the moment, they needed to get to the shelter of Sarah's house.

"Sarah," he whispered. "We need to go."

She turned to him and swiped away tears with her mitten. She nodded and got to her knees, then helped Lyddie before she stood.

"*Mamm*, are we safe?"

Sarah looked long at John, but all he could do was shrug. He wasn't going to lie, and he honestly didn't know if they were safe. All he knew was that they shouldn't stay there.

She put an arm around Lyddie and simply said, "We need to get home."

"May we have hot chocolate?" The girl's lower lip trembled.

Sarah seemed to force a smile for her child. "*Jah*. For sure and for certain."

"Ready?" John waited for an affirmative nod from Sarah and then turned to lead them back toward the house.

He stepped forward at a brisk pace, checking to make sure Sarah and Lyddie were following all right. Their big problem was the snow. More was coming, but until it covered their tracks, John didn't want to lead their would-be killer right back to Sarah's house. He detoured farther into the woods, stomping his feet and spreading the snow out. He circled around a tree and then a grouping of bushes and then another tree.

John motioned to Sarah. "Stay directly behind me. We don't want to leave three sets of prints in the snow, now that he—whoever *he* is—knows that there are three of us."

"*Jah*," Sarah agreed.

Whatever shelter of brush was available, John led them behind it. If the snowmobiler did return, John didn't want to be caught out in the open. Farther and farther from the crash site they marched, and all was quiet. The huffing and puffing had become more pronounced behind him, and John himself could use a breather. He slowed his pace to allow Sarah and Lyddie to rest.

Several minutes later, they emerged from the tree line and into the yard. Sarah and

Lyddie headed straight for the back door, untying their winter bonnets and shaking the snow off their capes before they entered.

John remained outside and surveyed the edge of the property. All seemed untouched. The snowmobiler had certainly gotten a good look at Sarah, but that didn't automatically mean that he knew where she lived or where to find them. Could they be safe now?

Sarah's home looked like all the other Amish homes in the area. Two stories with an attic rose whitewashed above an immaculate yard, at least what he could see under the snow. Red paint adorned the large barn, a striking contrast against the winter whiteness. He imagined that in the spring flowers would stand in neat rows, and he pictured Lyddie and Snowball playing on the green grass in the yard. Sarah's home was orderly inside and out. John wondered if the cliché "A place for everything and everything in its place" had originated with the Amish.

At the back door, John removed his hat and hung it on a hook. He secured the lock and stood for a moment, letting the warmth of the woodstove-heated home seep into him. Sarah busied herself at the counter, scooping cocoa powder into three mugs. Her face was rosy from the snow, and her natural beauty shone forth, framed by the rich brown of her hair.

Steam began to pour out of a kettle on the stove top. "Come. Sit. It will be ready in a jiffy." Sarah motioned him to the table, her hand trembling. "You need good food. Comfort food with nutritional value. To heal, *jah*?"

He crossed the kitchen to her and grasped her hands in his. Perhaps that would stop the shaking. "You were scared. Are scared. You don't have to fix a meal."

"I do, *jah*. When I am scared, I cook. When I am worried, I cook. When I am happy, I cook. It soothes."

He nodded his understanding and lowered himself to a chair.

She busied herself at the countertop, cutting thick slices of what looked like homemade bread. "You like tuna salad? Chicken noodle soup, also?"

Did he? He had no idea, but the simmering concoction in the pot on the stove top gave off an incredible aroma. "Um, sure."

As she continued the lunch preparations, John let his gaze wander the open living room. It was so quiet he could hear the satisfying squish of tuna salad being spread on bread, Lyddie's soft whisper as she sounded out words in her book, even his own breathing. He tapped his finger on the table, not surprised that he could hear it thumping on the wood. The silence was unnerving and yet pleasant at the same time. A man could do some serious thinking in that sort of solitude. But did he want to?

A side table with a lamp on top and a lower shelf filled with books and newspapers next to a plush blue recliner caught his attention. "Do you read much?"

"*Ach, jah.* I love to read. Lyddie and I visit the library on a regular schedule."

"What's your favorite?"

"I read all kinds. Cooking books, quilting, books about faith, even the good romance novels. Without television or a computer, I have more time for reading." She glanced at him while stirring the soup. "Do you enjoy reading?"

Did he? He picked up the book resting on the table, something with forgiveness in the title, and held it in his hands. It felt sturdy and comfortable there. He lifted it to his face and inhaled the scent of the paper, closing his eyes to try to picture himself somewhere, anywhere, with a book in his hands. But his mind was a blank. "I don't know, but I hope my new self, whoever I am now, likes to read."

Sarah nodded, a shy smile on her face. "Why not just decide that you do?" She placed two plates on the table and returned to the counter for the third. "Would you like a chocolate-chip cookie after lunch? Cookies are always a help in distress, *jah*?"

"Jah," he agreed, the foreign word a tingle on his tongue.

Distress. He had certainly brought plenty to this peaceful and peace-loving Amish household. It was all his fault, and what made it worse was that he had no idea why he was in trouble. Would prayer help? Perhaps. Was he a believing man? Maybe. Something stirred in him at the idea of praying to an almighty God. He bowed his head, but all he could summon was *Lord, help.*

The sound of Lyddie dropping a book on the floor startled him out of his attempt. She picked it up and settled herself on the sofa, apparently prepared to read until the refreshments were ready. John looked again around the room. Plain white walls, graced only by a calendar and clock, and a lack of knickknacks did nothing to detract from the warmth and welcome of the home.

Was all safe now? It was a question at the forefront of his mind, although there wasn't much else crowding the space in his brain. It was also the question he supposed Sarah would ask soon. How he would answer he had no idea, except that it seemed the man on the snowmobile had seen only Sarah and Lyddie. Perhaps he might just think they were curious about the wreckage.

But at least for this moment, he would sit still and be calm and recuperate. He didn't know anymore what future moments would hold just as he didn't know what past moments had held, so he would live right now, in this moment of warmth and light and safety.

"Lyddie, come quickly," Sarah called. The two joined John at the table, and Sarah and Lyddie bowed their heads for silent prayer. John bowed his head and tried to thank God for the food and the warm home, looking up again after Sarah said *amen*.

The child ate quickly, and Sarah suggested she go to her room to practice her stitching. The two hugged for a moment, and Sarah tucked a stray curl behind Lyddie's ear. As the girl passed John, she impulsively reached out to hug him. Her squeeze was tight and fast, and it infused John with a fondness that didn't feel familiar to him.

As soon as Lyddie was gone, Sarah turned

piercing eyes on John. "Who was that in the woods, and why was he shooting at us?"

Both valid questions. Questions for which he had no answers. "I wish I knew, but I can't even remember my own name. I certainly can't remember anyone else's name." He shrugged his shoulders. "I have no idea who that man was, but he seemed only to see you and Lyddie. Being at the site of the accident probably didn't help us."

"And you were dressed in the Amish clothing. Would that not help hide you?"

John thought back to what he had on. "Yes, I had an Amish coat on. My hat, which looked Amish, had come off, but it was nearby. But, I don't have the beard that most Amish men have." He scruffed his hand over his jaw. "Just a little stubble. Still, though, that could be enough to disguise me."

"Are we in danger?" Sarah hugged her arms around her middle.

He couldn't answer *yes* or *no* to that question. But he could advise caution. "I'm not sure. But we need to be careful. Even though I have no idea who that man was that shot at us, and he didn't see me, he saw you. I'm grateful he was scared off by that car that drove by." He would be back, though, just at a more opportune time.

* * *

Sarah's hands trembled as she picked up her plate and glass and placed them in the sink. "Will he be able to find us here?"

She glanced around her home, the one she had shared with her husband, the one that held so many memories with Lyddie. Was there a threat right outside the blue-shaded windows, a threat that would come bursting through and alter her life?

"You don't know him, right?"

"No, I have never seen him."

"Then he's probably not familiar with the Amish around here. At least not to the point where he knows who you are and where you live." John stood and carried his plate to the sink. "I think we're all right for now."

For now. But John's memory was gone. He didn't know his name or his occupation or even what sort of person he was. Could she trust him to be vigilant? To be protective if necessary? To know what to do?

She ran water in the sink and added soap while John continued to clear the table. At least he was a helpful sort. What woman wouldn't appreciate that? And so far, he had been courteous and thoughtful.

He placed the last dish on the counter and

smiled. "Do you have a cloth? I'll wipe up the table."

Ach, he was handsome, too, with that dark brown hair that seemed to stand up in all directions and his green eyes the color of fresh grass in the spring. He was the opposite of her blond-headed Noah, but now that he was dressed like a proper Amish man? She would need to guard her heart carefully.

She handed him a dishcloth and plunged her hands back into the hot water. How could she ever think that way about him? First of all, her husband, the love of her life, had passed just two years ago. How could she be untrue to his memory? And second of all, John was an *Englischer*. An outsider. She would never agree to be unequally yoked. How could she be so selfish as to even consider John? *Gott* had allowed her husband to be killed in the buggy accident. Thus, it must be *Gott*'s will that she be alone. She would embrace the will of *Gott*, no matter what misery may come her way.

John returned the cloth to her, and she rinsed it and hung it over the faucet. "Your last name, Burkholder, is it a common Amish name?"

"Are you wondering how easily this bad

man might be able to ask around and find us? But how would he know my name?"

He stuffed his hands in his pockets, stretching the suspenders. "Just trying to figure it all out."

"Burkholder is somewhat common in northern Indiana. But not so much, yet, that we all need nicknames like in other Amish communities where there are multiple men with the same name."

"Do you have family nearby?"

She retrieved a clean drying cloth from a drawer and prayed to *Gott* that she wouldn't need it to dry her tears. "I grew up in Lancaster County in Pennsylvania. My husband, Noah, thought the area was becoming overcrowded and moved us to Indiana for more job opportunities and land to build a house and barn. So, no, I do not have family nearby. My family remains in Pennsylvania, although they do come to visit from time to time."

"Have you thought of moving back?"

She eyed the letter from her mother that still rested on the windowsill. "Yes." That was all the answer she could summon.

He leaned one hip against the counter, and the fresh smell of the woods in winter wafted toward her. "What about a telephone? What would you do in case of an emergency?"

She twisted the towel in her hands. Sarah had never thought herself isolated, but when this *Englischer* started asking his questions, doubts began to ping in her mind, especially with no husband handy. "Since we are close to the edge of the state park, the area is heavily wooded. We are on the outskirts of the Amish community, and neighbors are scarce. My husband preferred the seclusion. There are some *Englisch* houses on the main road, but they are quite a distance, especially in the snow, and they are in the opposite direction of our church district. Our closest neighbor has a telephone in his barn for his business, but he is a couple of miles away. I can use it when I need it, and then I pay my part of the bill to him."

"You never thought of having your own phone?"

"My husband and I talked about it, for our barn, but it did not seem that necessary since the neighbor had one." She glanced at him as he pulled back the window blind a fraction of an inch and glanced out. "That must seem odd to you."

John turned to her with a wry chuckle. "Everything seems odd right now."

Of course it does. How could she be insensitive? Her troubles were nothing compared to what John was going through. "Our church district is currently considering cell phones, just the old kind that flip open. No internet. But it has not yet been decided."

"Any chance that'll happen soon?"

"No. A new rule needs to be approved unanimously, and some are still doubtful. It could take a long time." She stacked the plates in the cabinet and hung up the towel. "I cannot think what I would need it for, except maybe emergencies."

John opened his mouth to answer, but the sound of her gravel driveway crunching under the tires of a car that had turned into her lane kept him silent.

Should she duck out of sight? Turn off the lamp? Her mind felt paralyzed, and all she could do was grip the edge of the countertop as she watched John peer through a slit in the curtain.

It must have been only a second before he turned to her. "It's the sheriff's car."

The sheriff? The man who had never been helpful but only trouble for the Amish? Was he here for John? Did that mean that John was a bad guy...or a good guy? She spun to scan the room. Lyddie remained upstairs, the best place for her right now.

Sarah stared at John, waiting for an instruction. But he sat very still, as if not wanting to show his own alarm. Perhaps he was trying to think of what to do.

He jumped to his feet, and she stepped back, startled at his sudden movement. With a look toward the back door, he said, "Step out the back way and meet him in the driveway around the front. Be friendly, but don't let him in the house. Just in case." He pointed to the window near the front door. "I'll be concealed right behind that curtain, and I should be able to hear everything that's said. Can you do that?"

With a nod, she grabbed her cape from the hook and slung it over her shoulders. A glance back as she opened the door revealed John at the window already, pulling the curtain aside. "You'll be fine." He coupled the encouragement with a grin.

She had no idea whether he truly felt that way or not, but it was good to hear.

Outside, she stepped carefully off the porch and inhaled deeply of the cold air, letting the chill cut through her lungs. It revived her, and she prayed for *Gott*'s help as she stepped toward the Sheriff's vehicle. "Sheriff Jaspar. What can I do for you?"

The sheriff stepped forward from his driver's-side door, a tall, lanky man whose uniform hung on him. He pushed his wire-rimmed glasses farther up on his nose, although they seemed nearly embedded in his eyes already. "Mrs. Burkholder, isn't it?" He quickly adopted a quizzical look.

"*Jah*. That is correct."

"There's been a report of smoke in the area, and I'm making the rounds, just checking it out."

Sarah tightened her arms closer to her under her cape and snuck a glance at the front window. John's snowmobile crash had created lots of smoke. "Is anyone burning their rubbish?"

The sheriff stepped closer, so close that Sarah could see the little pattern on the rim of his glasses. "No. Not that I've found yet. And it's not the smoke from a fireplace or woodstove. Curious thing, really, and awfully close to your house."

Sarah took a small step backward. She desperately needed some distance from the man but didn't want to antagonize him. "I have only my heating stove."

Jaspar closed the gap between them. "Shall I come in and make sure?" He laid his claw-like hand on her arm.

A loud gasp escaped her and echoed through the winter silence. Before she could respond to the sheriff, the front door flung open. John stepped out, one hand fisted around his suspenders.

The sheriff turned to see who it was and immediately stepped back from Sarah. His gaze seemed to travel up and down John's height and back and forth the width of John's shoulders. He took another step back.

"Sarah?" John's intensity pierced her, and she nodded slightly to indicate that she was all right. He probably didn't dare to speak any more, not with his *Englisch* accent.

Sheriff Jaspar straightened his hat and then nodded at John. "Is this your brother? I've heard you have family in Pennsylvania that come to visit on occasion."

She wouldn't lie, but she did not see the need to tell the whole truth either. "*Jah*, I have family in Lancaster County." She fluttered her hand to her throat and swallowed hard. "He is visiting for a while."

The sheriff seemed satisfied as he edged back toward his car. "Well, I have a deputy looking into the smoke, as well. No need to worry, but let me know if there's any trouble." A roguish smile crawled across his face. "I'll keep you up-to-date."

She raised a hand in goodbye and quickly joined John at the front door. He opened it for her, and she stepped inside while he remained outside, his hand on the knob of the open door, staring hard at the sheriff as he backed out of the drive.

Her hands shook as she removed her cape and turned away from the door to sink into a chair at the kitchen table. John closed and locked the door then lowered himself into a matching chair.

The cape draped over her lap warmed her quickly, but she couldn't stop the trembling. She glanced at John, but he stared at the wall, seemingly lost in thought. "You are exposed now. You have been seen."

A few moments passed, then he tore his gaze from the straightforward direction and looked at her. There was a hard edge to his expression, yet it was tinged with compassion. "I couldn't just leave you out there with him. I saw everything through the window."

She smoothed out the tablecloth with the palm of her hand. "The sheriff is new and does not know how to get along with the Amish. What can I do?"

"Depending on what he finds out about the smoke that's been reported, you can pack your bags and prepare to leave."

"Leave?" Her hands seemed to act independently, and she found herself smoothing more of the cloth at a furious rate.

"Yes. We need to think about where we might be able to hide, just in case there is danger." He paused. "I've wondered if I should just leave. Perhaps you would be safe again if I was gone. But the problem with that is that he has seen you. He pointed his weapon at you."

"But the sheriff, if he finds what caused the smoke, could find the men who chased you. Perhaps we should help him and tell him what happened."

He clasped her hands in his. "But you don't trust the sheriff, and after what I saw and heard just now, I agree with you. That's not the proper behavior of a law-enforcement officer."

"Then perhaps we can contact someone else. I can hitch up the buggy and we can drive to the telephone." Her hands were warm in his, and she had no desire to leave her home, whether it be to hide or to seek help. She wanted just to stay here, with John holding her hands. How long had it been since a physical touch had communicated such comfort?

"I'm just not sure who we can trust." He removed a hand from hers and ran it through his hair. "I'm not sure of anything. And I don't want to make the situation worse."

Sarah glanced around the room and listened to the sounds of her only child playing in the room above her. She had a responsibility to the girl as well as to everything she and her husband had worked for. The sheriff was involved now, but did that make her feel any safer? The only man who had proven that he had a protective nature was the man sitting at her table. But he couldn't even remember who he was. What if, when he regained his memory, John was one of them?

FIVE

John needed two things. He needed a breath of fresh air. And he needed to remember.

Well, he needed a few other things, as well, like confidence that he had the instincts to protect the woman and her child, an assurance that all would end well and another piece of that amazing apple pie.

As Sarah had busied herself with baking something—he couldn't remember now what all she had said she was making, but apparently it was like therapy for her—he had tossed on the coat and, after a look around the yard to make sure there was no trouble, headed to the barn to explore a bit.

He swung the door open and stepped into the warmth, filling his lungs with the scent of hay. With the door closed behind him, he searched the nooks and crannies of his mind to see if the scent of the barn felt familiar.

Was he a farming man? An outdoors enthusiast? An animal lover?

Nothing came into his mind. It was as blank as a washed blackboard.

In different circumstances, the loss of his memory could have been an interesting opportunity to remake his life. The disappearance of his memories included not only the good ones but also the bad ones. Was he at odds with someone in his life? With no memory of it, he could approach the relationship with a fresh perspective.

Under these circumstances, though? In the house was a woman and her daughter who needed his protection from danger he had brought to their doorstep, no matter what he could or could not remember. Three lives depended on him.

A tabby cat mewed and rubbed against his legs. He bent to scratch it between the ears. Was he a cat person? He had no idea, but this one sure was cute. A mouse skittered along the wall, and the cat crouched down, its fur standing at attention along its back. The cat crept toward the mouse and pounced, catching it under its paw. John watched the cat play with and torment the mouse for a moment. When the cat took the mouse into its mouth and sauntered away, John wandered farther into the barn.

The sheriff had not been reassuring in the least bit, and that drove John to search for something—anything—helpful. Weapons? Although he wasn't sure what, or if he would know how to use it if he found anything. Hiding places? But how complex could a barn be? Anyone familiar with living in the country would know where to look. Memories? He grinned to himself at the irony of looking for memories in a new and unfamiliar place.

Sarah had made it clear that the Amish were a nonviolent people, so he didn't expect to find any weapons in the barn. It didn't have to be a gun, though, that could provide some defense. Perhaps a tool would do.

A door stood to his right. He had to push hard on the latch to get it open, and the hinges squeaked as he pushed. Clearly, it hadn't been opened in a while.

Large windows let the afternoon sunshine spill in, dust motes dancing in the still air. A large wooden table filled the middle of the space, and the other walls were filled with shelves of tools and piles of wood. He had found a woodworking shop, and it looked as if nothing had been touched for quite some time. He wandered toward a board that lay on the bench and ran his hand over the smooth wood. Someone had taken quite a bit of time to sand it well. A stack of rough-cut lumber sat on a shelf to the side, but he knew better than to run his hand over the wood full of splinters. It looked to be oak, but he had no idea how he knew that.

A block plane lay on a shelf, and he hefted it in his hand, the smooth and worn handle resting in his palm. It felt right there, but it wouldn't do much good as a weapon. Did he have a woodworking background? Confusion riddled his brain, yet it mixed with the pleasure of knowing that something felt right to him.

A child's step stool rested on the workbench. Stain had darkened it to a rich brown, and a can of polyurethane sat nearby. A brush rested on top of the can. It looked as if that was all that was left to finish the stool.

He picked up the brush and turned it around in his hand. A sense of satisfaction filled him, a pleasure in craftsmanship.

He was learning a little bit about himself already, in just these few minutes spent in the barn. Apparently, he liked to work with his hands. Had he learned about woodworking in a high school shop class? From his father? An image flashed through his mind, so strong and so startling that he closed his eyes to block out distraction. It was the vision of hands using a brush on paper. Were those his own hands? Strident voices had filtered in from another room, but what were they discussing so fervently?

He opened his eyes and looked down at his hands as he held the brush. Were they the same? Who were the people, and what were they arguing over? He closed his eyes again to return to the memory, but it was gone. Only a vague unsettled feeling of wrongdoing lingered.

His hand closed in a tight grip over the paintbrush. Why couldn't he remember? Whatever it was, whatever had been right there, even for a split second, seemed crucial. But why? John threw the brush on the table and took a deep breath.

Anger wouldn't solve anything.

"John?" Sarah's sweet voice filtered through the stillness of sawdust and afternoon sunlight and dancing dust motes.

"I'm in here." He quickly straightened the can and the brush. Why did he feel like a child who had been caught with his hand in the cookie jar?

Sarah appeared in the doorway, the light

blue of her dress fairly glowing in the sifted sunshine. Upset stretched across her face.

He stepped to her, his heart beginning a worried thump. "What's happened? I said you should stay in the house with the doors locked."

"All is well inside." Her gaze swept across the room and came to rest on the little stool. "What are you doing in here? With that?"

"I…uh…" John glanced back at the stool, which now seemed to incriminate him in some way. When he turned back, Sarah's eyes puddled with tears. "I was looking around. This looked like it might be the right size for Lyddie."

"Jah." She swiped at her cheek. "It was to be for Lyddie. This was my husband's workshop. I haven't been in here since he died."

The reality of the situation slammed him, and he gulped in air. Her husband had been a carpenter, and the stool had been his project at the time of his death. "I'm sorry. I didn't know."

Sarah walked to the workbench and fingered the edge. "My husband made furniture, the Amish furniture that *Englischers* love so much, for stores in the big cities like Indianapolis, Chicago, even Cincinnati and Louisville. This was where he worked."

He had overstepped his bounds and hurt her. Being in here was difficult enough for her, but to see him with one of her husband's projects, a project for her daughter? How could he make it up to her? Make it right?

"I'm sorry." He would say it a dozen times if that would help. "You've done so much for me. I wanted to do something for you."

She nodded, then covered her face with her hands. Her shoulders shook, and John saw a tear escape.

He longed to close the distance between them and comfort her, but did he dare? How would she receive it? Would it only make the situation worse?

Sarah gave up trying to hide her tears and hugged herself instead, but how much better that comfort would be if it were a strong man's arms around her. Reassuring. Soothing. Consoling.

Ach, but *Gott* had taken away her husband. That had been His will. So be it. But how she suffered since his death! Still, though, had not the bishop just preached about *Gott* comforting in sorrow? About praising Him through the difficult times? Well, she would obey. A verse sprang to her mind as she rubbed her hands over her arms. *Blessed be God, even the Father of our Lord Jesus Christ, the Father of mercies, and the God of all comfort.*

Jah, blessed be *Gott*.

John apologized again, breaking her reverie. The look of misery on his face matched the misery she felt in her heart. He stepped toward her, seemingly unsure of what to do next.

"It is all right," she whispered into the space between them.

Despite the cold outside, it was warm in the barn. John had removed his coat and rolled his sleeves up. He reached out and touched her gently on the forearm, then withdrew his hand as if he felt the same zing on his skin as she felt through her sleeve.

As Sarah sniffed the last of her tears, she watched John return the tools to their places. The muscles in his forearms rippled as he hefted the large can of polyurethane and placed it on the shelf with some other containers. Of course, she had been treating his wounds and changing the bandage on his arm where he got cut on the rocks. But that was simply medical care of an injured person. Now, to see him standing solid and in good physical condition, he was strong and handsome.

Guilt stabbed her in the heart. *Gott* would

never want her to be unequally yoked with an *Englischer*. She had no business looking at him as anything except a fellow human being who needed some help temporarily. Maybe she did need a husband and her daughter needed a father. For sure and for certain, she wanted to be married again and have more *bobblin*. Many more babies.

But if that was the will of *Gott*, He would bring her the right husband in His time.

John pushed the little step stool to the center of the workbench, then turned to her. "Is that better? I don't want to be the cause of any further difficulties. I won't come in here again."

Sarah swiped one last rogue tear from her cheek, the twisting of her heart slowing. The scent of wood and sawdust filled the barn, but it seemed also to waft particularly from John. It was the scent of hard work and masculinity.

It was the scent of misery.

This dance was difficult, and John didn't know the steps.

With everything back in its place, Sarah seemed to calm a bit, but John still wondered if he should comfort her further. How would he be received? And what was this attraction he had for this beautiful plain woman?

He touched her upper arm, gently, questioningly, and she simply smiled. *"Danki."*

She turned and strode into the main part of the barn. John followed and closed the door securely behind him.

"Did you find what you were looking for?"

John chuckled. "I'm not sure I know what I'm looking for. Just exploring."

"Would you like some coffee? To warm you?"

One of the horses whinnied, and the cat returned to rub against the hem of Sarah's long skirt.

The door burst open, and John bounded in front of Sarah. His pulse throbbed in his arteries at the rush of adrenaline. He had allowed himself to be lulled into a sense of security, in the warmth and comfort of the barn. But he needed to be alert at all times.

Frigid air slammed into his face. Lyddie stood in the doorway, a caped and bonneted silhouette against the light outside. *"Mamm?* I came downstairs, and you were not there."

Sarah pulled Lyddie into a hug. "I am sorry, little one. I was out here with John."

The girl looked up, her round cheeks framed with blond wisps of hair, her *kapp* like a beacon of innocence over it all. John's heart twisted within his chest at the sight of mother and daughter. He longed for the love and acceptance of family. Did he have it and just not know it?

Lyddie stepped away from her mother, an adorable and impish expression gracing her face. "May I have a snack?"

"We just had lunch. Are you hungry again already?"

Mother and daughter stepped toward the door, ready to return to the house.

"Just a minute." John lunged toward the closest stall and dodged a flick of a horse tail. A pitchfork rested against the wall, waiting for the next time for chores. It would have to do for now, with nothing else available. He hoisted it in his hand, the solid wooden handle fitting snuggly in his palm. "Let me check outside first. Just to be safe."

He sidestepped around the pair and pulled his coat on. He surveyed the yard but without stepping completely outside. The winter wind whipped around the side of the house, stirring the snow into a whirlwind that skipped over the frozen ground. Mournful gray clouds now filled the sky. A storm was approaching quickly.

John led them across the yard and back to the house, the pitchfork pointed forward. He wasn't sure how he might explain that to the sheriff if he returned, but he would figure something out if necessary. His continual scan of the area didn't reveal any present threats.

But that didn't mean they weren't there, in the shadows, biding their time, waiting for the opportune moment.

Inside the house, he locked the door and leaned the pitchfork against the wall.

At the ready.

Just in case.

SIX

The afternoon had brought only more cloud cover, and sunset had seemed to come early. Flurries of snow had begun as Sarah had returned to the barn to bed down the two horses, Thunder and Lightning, for the night. Now, as Sarah looked out the small barn window, fat, fluffy flakes of snow traipsed down to add a fresh layer. Snowball panted at her side, ready to go wherever she went.

John stood at the door. He had been waiting patiently, helping as he could, and now was ready to escort her back to the house. With pitchfork in hand, he had prowled the perimeter of her property to make sure all was safe. The farming implement remained at the ready, but with no present threat, he seemed a little more relaxed. "Done?"

"Jah." She turned back toward the hayloft. "Lyddie! Time to go back to the house!"

The six-year-old clambered down the ladder as Snowball left Sarah's side to prance around at the bottom, her tail conveying her enthusiasm.

Sarah's heart beat the staccato rhythm that had become her new normal as John opened the door and surveyed the yard. There was nothing normal about it, though, and she prayed to *Gott* that this danger would be over soon.

"Is all well?" She peeked over his shoulder, inhaling the scent of sawdust and wood, but all she could see was the serenity of a snowfall on a winter's night.

"Seems so."

For now. That's what he wasn't saying.

"I'm trying my best to remember. So that I can get back to my life and get out of your way." He stepped out into the snow, and Snowball ran in front, her nose turned up to the snowflakes. "I'm sorry for all this."

"*Jah.* It will come in time."

"If I had any idea of who had attacked us earlier, I might be better able to know how we could defend ourselves. But I don't know who he is or what he wants."

There it was again, the talk about self-defense. Sarah put her hand on his arm. Perhaps the gesture would help calm him. "You know that self-defense is not the Amish way."

"I know. I know. I know what you've already said. But I'm not Amish, and I'll defend myself, and you and Lyddie, if necessary."

Sarah removed her hand and stuffed it in the pocket of her cape, checking on Lyddie to make sure she was following behind. An ache rose to throb in her chest, but she refused to examine why a wave of loneliness invaded her soul. She was Amish. John was not. She forced her thoughts to stop right there.

He would do what he needed to do, and she would do what she needed to do. In the end, she would be grateful if her life was spared, and the life of her daughter. But if it was *Gott*'s will that her time had come, she would do her best to accept it graciously.

Snow gathered on their shoulders, on John's hat and Lyddie's *kapp*, as Snowball bounded alongside. The animal licked her hand as if trying to reassure her.

Halfway there, Snowball's exuberance came to a halt. A branch snapped to their left. The malamute's ears stood at attention, and then she began a low growl as she eyed the tree line. John swung out his arm to stop them. They stood like statues, listening and squinting into the darkness. The pitchfork pointed toward the sound.

The ache in Sarah's chest increased with her heart rate. A thousand different scenarios raced through her mind. Was this what John had been afraid of? Had the man in the snowmobile suit, with the scary bruising and the gun, finally found them? And the worst question of all—how would a pitchfork protect them against a bullet?

"To the house." John's strident whisper broke the silence. "Quickly."

Sarah grabbed Lyddie's hand. Together, they picked up their skirts and galloped toward the back door as quickly as their winter boots would allow. John followed close behind, his hand at the small of Sarah's back, urging her along.

At the door, John pushed her and Lyddie inside along with Snowball. "I'll check around. Lock the door, and don't open it until you see me."

She nodded her assent and closed the door behind him. Lyddie dropped to her knees to hug the dog. Desperate to do something with her hands, Sarah unfastened her cloak while she watched through the window as John disappeared into the darkness. A few moments later, his face appeared in the pane. She quickly unlocked the door for him.

As he hung his hat on the peg, Sarah locked the door behind him. He leaned against the wall and rubbed his temples. "Nothing. I saw nothing."

Sarah inhaled a large breath to clear away the anxiety. "Is your head hurting again?"

"A little." He hung his coat on the hook and resumed massaging his forehead.

"Why not sit down for a spell? Perhaps it will ease your headache. If you can feel better, it will help us all."

He nodded. "Maybe, but I'll be right in there—" he pointed toward the recliner in the living room "—and you call me if you need anything."

"*Jah*, I will."

As he retreated to rest, she instructed Lyddie to set the table. With her cape and bonnet on the hook, she quickly washed her hands and peeked into the propane-powered oven at the chicken she had put in before she had gone to care for the horses.

A couple of years ago, Sarah had doubted the choice of a malamute as a farm dog. Everything she had read indicated that they were not good guard dogs, often licking the hands of strangers rather than growling a warning. But her husband had wanted a strong dog, a work dog, and the malamute breed was nothing if not strong. Of course, once Lyddie had held the soft, furry puppy, the decision was made.

So, Snowball's warning outside had been a surprise, but perhaps not helpful in the end. They had feared an intruder when it had probably only been a deer searching for food. Now, Snowball settled into her bed on the back inside porch.

The chicken had browned nicely, and Sarah stood to lift the lid of the pot on the stove top. Chunks of potato simmered in the gently bubbling water. She retrieved a fork from the drawer and speared a piece of potato against the side of the pot. It resisted a little too much, but a few more minutes would finish them.

Unsettledness dogged her, and she licked her lips to ease the dryness as she reminded herself to keep a steady hand when taking the chicken from the oven. If only John were sitting at the table, would that ease her? It seemed that he had been there with his calming presence for a lot longer than just a couple of days. But that's all it had been since Lyddie had led her to the man bleeding into the snow near his wrecked snowmobile. She glanced at the table, eyeing what she had begun to think of as *his chair*. But she wouldn't bother him. He needed his rest, especially with his headache. Rest was always helpful in recovery, and she prayed that included recovery of memories.

She paced to the front window and peered out. But when she saw nothing but more nothingness, she pulled the curtain closed and double-checked to make sure the window was completely covered. She tested the lock on the front door, the cold of the metal sending a chill into her fingers. Her path took her through the living room, and John shifted in the chair as she passed. At the back inside porch, an attached but enclosed entryway without coverings on the windows, Snowball lay on her bed in the corner, raising her head for a petting when Sarah stepped in.

Lifting her long skirt out of the way, she crouched down to scratch behind the dog's ears. The malamute seemed almost to smile as Sarah spoke to her in her doggy voice. "Are you comfy, Snowball? Is it nap time? Are you tired from all your guarding?" She arranged the blanket around her, gave her one last scratch on top of her head and pushed herself to standing.

In the kitchen, Sarah thrust her hands into the oven mitts that rested on the countertop and removed the lid of the pot of potatoes into the sink. As she hefted the pot to carry it to the sink to drain the potatoes, Snowball whined from the back inside porch. Normally, she would not have noticed, but since John had arrived, her senses had been on full alert. Snowball had not been acting like herself either, which gave Sarah pause.

Still holding the pot, she approached the door to the porch to check on the dog, a reassuring sound on her lips. But as she entered the doorway, a man's scowling face stared in from the window.

She froze, her hands gripping the handles of the pot. Her heart took up an instant beating against her rib cage, as if trying to break free.

The man seemed to be looking to her side. He had not seen her.

Gott, help!

Before she could think to move, the doorknob rattled. The man's face pointed toward the doorway. His stare caught her. She looked straight into the most evil eyes she had ever seen.

What should she do?

A split second later, the door flung open. A malicious winter wind swirled around her. As the man reached in toward her, a crowbar in his hand, she turned the pot up and heaved the contents toward him. The water and chunks of potato hit him squarely in the face and chest. Water splattered on the floor, and chunks of potato bounced against her shoes.

The man let loose a cry of agonizing pain. Sarah stepped back but held on to the pot, her mind reeling to figure out what she should do next. With his eyes shut in pain, he continued to advance through the porch toward Sarah.

John scrambled from the chair and made it to the doorway to the back porch as the man emitted a second shout of agony. He quickly assessed the situation—the man clawing at his eyes, obviously in great pain and unable to see, and the Amish woman with the gut instincts to use a pot of boiling water as a weapon.

With both hands, John pushed the man back out the door. The intruder stumbled away, one hand on his face and the other hand out in front like a blind man trying to feel his way. He emitted a string of words that John was glad Sarah could not hear. Living a sheltered life as the Amish did, she may not even have known what they were.

John rushed back inside and locked the door. Sarah had returned to the kitchen, placing the pot in the sink and then standing, staring as if in shock. Lyddie peeked from behind the doorway, her eyes wide and her hands worrying the ties that hung loose from her *kapp*.

Not for the first time, John felt a desperation for a telephone. There was simply no way to summon help, except for hitching up the horse and buggy. But what help would he summon? The lack of knowledge was more crippling than the lack of a phone.

"That was good thinking on your part, Sarah." As he approached, she turned, her eyes puddled with unshed tears.

"*Gott*, forgive me. But I was so scared. I… I just reacted."

He laid his hand on her forearm and squeezed, a gesture he hoped conveyed his appreciation in her actions that had protected them all. "He'll be helpless for a while. His eyes were turning bright red and beginning to swell. But it's just a matter of time before he's back, probably with a vengeance."

Lyddie shrank against the wall. Snowball finally had emerged from her bed and came to Lyddie's side to lick her hand. "*Mamm*, are we going to die?"

Something seemed to shake free in Sarah, and her eyes focused on her daughter. Without heed to the windows or doors, she rushed across the kitchen and dropped to her knees in front of Lyddie, gathering her in her arms. "*Ach, liebchen.* We have John to protect us."

Both females looked to him with pleading eyes. John felt helpless enough on his own, with no memory and all experiences erased from his mind. But he couldn't let down this mother and daughter. Perhaps now was a good time to start praying. From what he had heard from Sarah over the past days, even though he didn't know who he was, God still knew everything about him, even down to the number of hairs on his head.

He embraced them both and impulsively planted a kiss on the girl's forehead. Then, taking a few steps backward, he grabbed the pitchfork from its resting place near the door, tossing up a prayer for protection and guidance. "Right. We need to get out of here. Whoever that was at the door, he'll be back. There's no way to tell how soon. It just depends on how much the boiling water hurt him and how soon his vision returns."

Sarah nodded, the tiny lines around her eyes seeming to ease a bit as John spoke. "A friend in a neighboring church district was canning last fall when the boiling water bubbled and burst up into her face. She was blinded temporarily, but she said the pain was intense. This water had cooled a little, and I do not think enough water hit him in his eyes to blind him permanently."

"Okay. So, pack a bag, Sarah, quickly. Grab the essentials. A change of clothes. Your toothbrushes. I don't know yet where we're going or how long we'll be gone."

He looked to Lyddie. She raised her head from her mother's shoulder, a crease on her cheek from the tie of Sarah's *kapp*. "Lyddie, get whatever your mother will allow you to take. Not too much. Just, perhaps, a favorite doll or a blanket."

The two stood and began to move toward the stairs, but John had one last instruction. "Turn out the kerosene lamp. We'll work in darkness. If he returns before we can leave, I don't want him to be able to see in. I'm going to grab some water and snacks. Be back down here in two minutes."

A quick peek out the window revealed that their attacker had not yet returned. John set the pitchfork aside and retrieved some bottles of water and little bags of snacks. Was he surprised that the Amish would buy prepackaged food? They shopped at the grocery stores just like everyone else. Whatever he thought, he didn't have time to examine it now. One thing he did know about the Amish, or at least about this Amish woman, specifically, she was resilient. She might be scared or worried, but she wasn't crumbling. Strength and resolve adorned her. Her unwavering faith in God only added to her beauty.

Sarah and Lyddie returned quickly. With John leading, they dashed across the yard to the barn. Snowball followed, pushing snow around with her muzzle as she trotted behind. By the moonlight that filtered in through the barn windows, Sarah hitched Lightning to the buggy and tied Thunder to the back.

"Will we move faster if we leave the second horse here?" John couldn't remember knowing anything about horses. He would have to rely on Sarah's expertise now.

"I cannot leave him alone in the barn." Sarah hitched up her skirt and climbed into the buggy after Lyddie. "Not with that bad man on the loose. And no one will be here to care for him."

John only nodded and swung up into the buggy as Sarah gave a *tch-tch* to the horse. She called for Snowball, and they pulled out of the barn and into the empty yard, the malamute trotting alongside.

"The snow will muffle the sound of the horse and cover our tracks, *jah*?"

"Yes. It should."

The moonlight cast eerie shadows across the landscape, and snowflakes flittered down from scattered clouds. A shudder involuntarily coursed through him. Where would they go from here? Was there anybody out there who cared? In the unnerving quiet of the lonely night and with his memory erased, it didn't stretch his imagination to think that they were the only three people left on the face of the earth.

A tiny window at the side, about the size of his face, allowed him the smallest of views. Another window about the same size afforded a view out the back of the buggy. The light of the moon reflecting on the snow provided ample light as Sarah guided them onto the road. John peered through his window, trying to see behind, and strained to hear the slightest sound a car might make if one approached. At his instruction, Lyddie kept to the back corner of the buggy, away from the window. As she clutched her blanket and doll, John longed to wrap his arms around the adorable girl and soothe her, but she would be safer if he maintained his vigilance.

With all quiet out his side, John turned to Sarah. She held the reins loosely, but the skin was tight across her mouth. At least they had what Sarah had called the storm front on the buggy to keep the snow from pelting them in the face.

He spoke quietly. "Where do you think we should go?" He tapped the brim of his hat. "For obvious reasons, I'm drawing a blank on what our options are outside of your house."

She forced a small grin, but the tightness remained. "The Amish take care of each other. We believe the Bible calls us to live in community together. There are plenty of families who would take us in."

"That may be true, but I don't want to bring danger to them."

"*Jah*, you are right."

"To have someone innocent hurt because of my problems that I can't even remember? That's unacceptable. It's terrible enough that you and Lyddie have been dragged into this."

Sarah chewed on her lip. If their situation hadn't been so dire, if he could just remember who he was, if she wasn't Amish and he wasn't *Englisch*, it could have been romantic, a buggy ride on a moonlit, snowy night. But there were too many *ifs* to let that thinking continue.

"But we need to stay somewhere, if just for the night. I cannot let Lyddie sleep in the buggy. And it is cold." She pushed some loose hair off her forehead with one hand.

"My friend Katie would let us in any time of the night."

"Does she live nearby?"

"Near enough. It will take some time, but I would not have suggested it if we could not get there with Lightning and the buggy."

He peered out the window again and then returned to face Sarah. "How do you know her?"

"She is also a widow and has twin three-year-old girls, Ruth and Rebekah. She struggles on her own." Sarah paused and swallowed hard. "Like I do. We help each other out with chores. I was supposed to drop Lyddie at her house in the morning to help with her twins while I sold my and Katie's goods at the market."

"Okay. If you think that's best."

Lyddie had fallen asleep by the time they reached the friend's house. There had been no sign of their attacker, but Sarah had said she was sticking to the back roads. It had taken a little longer, but perhaps they had been safer.

John waited in the buggy with Lyddie as Sarah knocked on the door.

The young Amish woman answered quickly, and Sarah and her friend had a hushed conversation. A few minutes later, Katie disappeared and then returned with boots and her cape. She opened the barn, and Sarah hopped back into the buggy to drive the horses inside.

"What was her reaction?"

"She was surprised, but of course we are welcome to stay."

"Did you tell her everything?"

"*Jah.* She has met the new sheriff also and agrees that he is not helpful or friendly to us."

John sagged against his seat. So even though law enforcement seemed to be involved, investigating the cause of the smoke, it probably wouldn't help. He continued to be on his own, struggling to remember and find a resolution to the situation with a deadline he couldn't quite grasp looming closer. "If I didn't think you were in danger, I would just leave and take the danger with me."

"I cannot just let you loose. You do not know who you are or where you belong. Where would you go? *Ach*, no. I will take care of you until you are well."

Katie unhitched the horses and settled them in stalls, Snowball tagging along into the warmth of the barn. As Sarah carried her bag, John pulled Lyddie from the back of the buggy and settled her against his shoulder, carrying her into the house. The girl was a comfortable weight in his arms, and the ache for a family returned. He pushed it away as quickly as it arrived. As he settled them into the spare bedroom, Sarah and Lyddie said good night.

In the dark of the living room, John spread his blanket on the couch. He would be the only one on the first floor, protecting them all by sleeping closest to the only entrances to the house.

He toed off his shoes and laid down, pulling the quilt over him. The tick of the clock tocked against his ear, in time to the worries that ricocheted through his mind. For now, they were safe, and all was well.

For now.

But what would tomorrow bring?

SEVEN

Sharp sunlight struck Sarah in the face. A peek through one eye revealed that a tiny crack in between the curtain and the edge of the window was the culprit. She raised an arm to cover her eyes and collided with the form in the bed next to her.

"Ow, *Mamm*." Lyddie's mop of blond curls, unrestrained by her prayer *kapp*, stirred in closer. The quilt moved across her, pulling nearer to Lyddie.

Sarah inhaled deeply of the chilly morning air and exhaled slowly, letting her mind absorb all that had happened in the last forty-eight hours. For a moment upon awakening, she had not been able to identify where she was or how she got there. Was that how John felt all the time? Her heart pounded within her at sympathy for the man whose life had been erased, and she took a moment to utter a silent prayer for the restoration of his memories.

She hugged Lyddie tightly and then eased out of the bed. *Jah*, she had been tired. But if the sun was that bright and that high already, the day was disappearing while she lollygagged in bed.

But it was beginning well, safe and warm and with, she was sure, a hot and hearty breakfast soon. Maybe fresh-baked biscuits with a dollop of apple butter, eggs with cheese and bacon, juice, milk, coffee. How could a day not feel like a fresh start with that kind of nourishment at the beginning?

She gently eased the straight pins through the fabric to fasten her skirt to the bodice, then twisted her hair into its customary bun and fastened on her prayer *kapp* with bobby pins. How would the day end, though? Here at her friend's house? At home? Or at another location?

The fresh aroma of coffee forced the musings from her mind. She would take life one day at a time and recite to herself the verses from the psalms that had comforted her in both her move from Pennsylvania and her husband's death. *So teach us to number our days, that we may apply our hearts unto wisdom... O satisfy us early with Thy mercy; that we may rejoice and be glad all our days.* However many days she had left—and considering their present dangers, it seemed to be fewer and fewer—she would rejoice and be glad.

Her task for that day, in addition to keeping herself and Lyddie alive and well, should have been to get her goods to the market. Despite the help of the students' parents, her teacher salary just wasn't quite enough. The parents were generous with foodstuffs and firewood. Every week, it seemed, a pupil would bring a basket of apples or a fresh loaf of bread. But if she'd learned anything in the past few days with John, it was that the future was not certain. Any little bit of money saved would provide extra security. But her current circumstances did not allow for normal activities.

Leaning back over the bed, she rustled Lyddie. "Time to awaken, sleepy."

Lyddie groaned but began inching her way toward the edge of the bed.

In the kitchen, Sarah found John with the newspaper in one hand and a cup of coffee in the other. Katie stood at the stove top, a spatula in hand.

"That smells delicious." Sarah retrieved plates from the cupboard and quickly set the table. "Scrapple? Did you make it last night?"

"Jah." Katie nodded toward the stairs. "Will Lyddie be up soon? We are almost ready."

Sarah nodded.

The paper crinkled, and John looked toward the frying pan. "What's scrapple?"

Sarah smiled at her friend. "It is *wunderbar* for breakfast, made of pork scraps boiled down. Then we thicken the broth with flour until it is a paste. Add some seasoning and chill through the night in the loaf pan."

"In the morning, we fry slices in the skillet." Katie gestured toward the slices sizzling in the pan.

As Sarah poured milk for the children, Lyddie appeared on the stairs, a huge smile stretched across her face. "Scrapple? *Danki!*"

Breakfast passed quickly, and the pork dish won John's hearty approval. As they cleared the table and washed the dishes, Katie pulled Sarah aside. "I have been watching John. You said he does not know anything about himself. But do you not think he looks like *Mammi* Mary?"

Sarah inhaled sharply. "The doctor said the same."

"She is at market this morning, selling her baked and jar goods. Perhaps you should go see her."

"Jah, I will talk to John."

At the sound of his name, John approached from the living room with a detour to peer out the window. "Talk about what?"

"Both Katie and Dr. Jones have said that you resemble Mary Miller. She is an elderly widow without family in the community and like a *grossmammi* to me. She is not my real grandmother, but she could be. I wonder if we should go see her, if she might have some clue to your identity. She has been in Nappanee for a long time. She is at market this morning."

Katie turned to Sarah, thought knitting her brow. "Did she not have family that left the Amish church? What happened to them? I think she has mentioned something about Fort Wayne, but I just cannot remember."

John stroked the stubble on his chin and walked first to the front window to look out and then to the enclosed back porch to peer into the yard. "Yes, let's go. The market will be crowded, right? We should be safe there, in a public place."

"And the market may help you remember. There could be something familiar there, something you see or smell or hear. The doctor said that even health professionals do not understand much about amnesia, so anything could be helpful."

"Perhaps." But he didn't look hopeful.

Her friend laid a comforting hand on Sarah's arm. "But I will keep Lyddie while you go, *jah*? It will be better for her here."

"*Jah*. Lyddie will help with the twins, so you can get your work done."

"I will pray that you and John find some answers."

"Pray for our safety, as well."

John donned his coat and hat, and Sarah hugged Lyddie long and hard. "Be helpful. Be careful," she said, although she knew her daughter did not need the admonishment.

As Sarah tied the strings of her winter bonnet under her chin, John checked outside. When he was satisfied that all was secure, they stepped quickly to the buggy.

Sarah hitched her skirt and stepped up to the buggy seat. Her friend held out a dried-apple pie to her. "For *Mammi* Mary. Every conversation goes better over a piece of pie."

Sarah shifted her foot against the brake and clucked to Lightning. The buggy jerked forward. "*Danki*, Katie. 'Tis true. We will see you in a little while."

She hoped, but would they?

As her friend waved goodbye, Sarah faced forward and turned the buggy onto the road. "*Mammi* Mary makes the best hot cider in all of northern Indiana. She may have a thermos of it at market."

As Sarah guided Lightning, she warmed inside, but was it from the handsome man next to her or the thought of hot cider with lots of cinnamon?

If only it could be a leisurely drive. But John wouldn't allow himself to relax back into the seat. Instead, he repeatedly checked every window for approaching vehicles, whether automobile or snowmobile, his hand gripping the edge of the seat.

He was fairly certain he wasn't Amish, but he didn't know exactly what kind of life he had lived before the attack or the speed at which he conducted it. This pace, though? Being able to see the tree limbs burdened with snow and rabbit tracks in the fields? The clip-clop of the horse in front? He wished it could be tranquil. Rather, it was frustrating, being out in the open with no real option for a speedy getaway. He leaned forward on his seat and stuck his head out for a good look around. All was clear for that instant. But what would the next minute bring?

So far, amnesia had been equal parts disconcerting and comforting. He had had moments of panic, of sweaty palms and racing heart, not knowing who he was, where he lived, who his relatives were. Did he like asparagus? Had he had a good childhood? Were Christmases warm and enjoyable or lonely and agonizing?

But it was also oddly comforting. Whatever bad memories he had had, they were gone. Had he had an argument with someone? A falling out? A difficult moment? It was now all erased. He had a fresh beginning in front of him. He could be whoever he wanted to be.

His nose began to tingle from the cold, and he rubbed a gloved hand over it. This riding in an open buggy was not for those who easily chilled. Sure, they had the storm front, and a couple of heavy blankets were available in the back if he wanted one. For sure and for certain, as Sarah would say, the Amish were a hearty bunch. Yes, they were peaceful, but they had endurance.

He checked the windows again and listened carefully. The hum of a car engine sounded faintly in the distance. Through the side window, he scanned the horizon, but a small hill rose up and prevented much visibility. John's fists clenched as he waited for the vehicle to appear.

"A car?" Sarah's voice held a tremor of something. Apprehension?

"I think so. Just keep driving. Is there a turnoff coming up? Anywhere to go?"

"No. Nothing."

The humming became louder, and as the vehicle crested the rise, the sound became more of a rumble.

John pressed his face to the cold glass to see what was coming. A moment later, it slowed as it approached. A delivery truck with the name of a popular beverage passed the buggy, veering around them and into the other lane to make a wide berth.

Sarah's exhalation matched his own. Relief filled him, and John turned forward to see that she slumped against the seat. The sooner they arrived at the public marketplace to see *Mammi* Mary, the better.

They rode in silence, and Sarah's lips moved occasionally. He continued his vigil through the windows but needed a distraction. He hated to interrupt what was probably prayer, but a little more information about their destination would also be helpful.

He waited for a pause in the movement of Sarah's lips, a waiting that was not unpleasant as he studied her pert nose and the way her eyelashes fell gently on her pink cheeks. She must have sensed him watching, for she turned and narrowed her eyes at him. *"Jah?"*

"I just was wondering about *Mammi* Mary and how she came to be like a grandmother to you."

"Each church district is close. Close together in where they live and close together in relationship. That is one of the best benefits of being Amish."

"Right. I understand that. But you talk about her as if you have a special relationship with her."

"I guess I do. She is also from Lancaster, so we have that in common. Her husband died many years ago, and she has no other family. I think there was a child, but she does not speak of him or her."

"So, you're both alone here in Indiana?"

"Jah." She paused to swallow. John wanted to kick himself. Was it sadness that clogged her throat? "I have suggested that she move in with me, but she will not. She says that she is hoping I will marry again."

Now it was John's turn to swallow hard. "Marry? A nice young Amish man?" He didn't want to examine why that thought bothered him.

"Jah. Must be Amish."

John turned to stare out the window again, unable to think of a reply that wouldn't embarrass him.

* * *

Another car approached and drove around them, slowing as it passed. John held out his arm to motion her to lean back and watched for the people to come into view. Sarah's hands perspired in her gloves, and she tightened her grasp on the reins. As the car pulled forward, a young girl in the back seat held up her cellular phone and pointed it at them.

Sarah flung a hand to her face as she whispered to John, "Cover your face."

He immediately looked away and raised a hand to cover his eyes, nose and mouth. As the car passed on, John sagged back. "Not very polite, taking our picture like that, but at least they weren't the guys who are after us." He swiped his hand over his forehead and then straightened his hat. "Does that bother you?"

"We are used to it. And what *gut* purpose would that serve, being bothered?"

"None, I guess."

"And see? They thought you were Amish. The clothing helps you fit in."

"But it isn't really my own, just like the name John isn't mine. For the sake of safety, though, I'll keep both the name and the clothing."

As they approached an intersection just a

mile from the market, Sarah spotted a buggy coming from the right, followed closely by yet another buggy. Amish traffic was getting heavier as they neared the market. She glanced over at John. He had his arms crossed over his chest, even as he continued to survey the area and examine each vehicle that came into view.

Sarah pulled on the reins to halt Lightning at a four-way stop. After passing through, she turned to John. "You should drive."

He sat up straight. "What? Drive the horse and buggy?"

"*Jah.* We are getting more traffic, and it will look wrong if I am driving. It will draw attention to us." The very thought of drawing the wrong attention compelled her to check from side to side.

"I don't know anything about how to drive a horse and buggy."

"I will show you. It is not difficult." She suppressed a smile at the anxiety on his face. "You will learn quickly, I am sure. At the very least, you need to hold the reins in your hand, so we look like everyone else."

"Okay. But you know the last thing we need is a runaway horse and a buggy accident. Just stay close."

Sarah studied him for a moment. He was

awfully cute when he was nervous. And she would definitely stay close, for as long as he wanted her. "It would be worse if those bad men found us again, *jah*?" That sobering thought brought her attention back to the task at hand.

John didn't answer, which was probably wise, considering the tension of the moment. "So, what's first?"

"The first rule to remember is to never let go of the reins. You are in charge."

He nodded solemnly and held his hands to mimic hers.

"See how Lightning's ears are flicking back? He is listening for you to tell him what you want him to do."

"Do I need to tell him something now?"

"No, he is fine." Would John be fine, though? For being such a strong and protective man, he looked as skittish as a colt. "You will be fine, too. Just sit up straight and place your feet on that low front board to brace them." Sarah tapped the toes of her boots against the board.

At the sound, John glanced down and then arranged his feet on the board just as Sarah had hers. He would do well, being such a quick study. "Okay. What now?"

"Now you take the reins. Hold them between your middle and third fingers. Like this." She held her hand out to demonstrate.

With John holding his fingers in the proper position, Sarah placed the reins in between his fingers. As she released them into his grip, her hand swept across his, and she felt what was probably a jolt of electricity at the touch of his hand. She had never felt electricity or had electricity, but that was how the novels described it. Was that what this feeling was? It was a tingle that instantly *ferhoodled* her. It scared her, so maybe she should let go of his hand. But it also made her want to hold on because it thrilled her.

It must have been only a second or two, that touch. But she forced herself to let go. He was, after all, supposed to be the one driving the buggy.

John's skin burned where she had touched him. Soft, gentle Sarah.

It didn't last near long enough, and she jerked her hand away as if stung. Cold invaded suddenly, and he shivered in the vacuum left by her withdrawal.

Back to business. That's what his attitude should be. That's what his attitude should have been all along. It was not his business to be smitten by this sweet and soft yet surprisingly resilient Amish woman.

He gripped the reins with a ferocity that matched the tension he felt. This not-knowing had been interesting at first. A bit of a relief, really, as he realized that he couldn't remember bad memories either. But now he was at his wit's end. He had just enough information to know that there was something important—something bad—lurking in the recesses of his mind. But what was it? And how could he dredge it out?

"See? You are doing well." Sarah's voice brought him back to the present and the important task of driving the horse and buggy safely to market.

Something about her voice made him turn to her, and a gentleness seemed to radiate from her.

Would the market help him remember? Smells? Sights? Sounds? If he knew what would trigger a memory, he would remember already and wouldn't need to trigger the memory. It seemed to be a vicious circle. And if he was a man of faith, then shouldn't prayer be a part of his life?

"*Ach*, John, mind the horse."

He shook his head to clear away the fog of

thoughts to see that with a lack of attention to his driving, he had allowed Lightning to slow and wander off the side of the road. "I'm sorry. What do I do now?"

"Just cluck your tongue like this, and keep a light touch. *Tch-tch*, Lightning." The horse flicked his ears and headed back toward the road, picking up his pace. "He knows what to do, but he appreciates encouragement."

John adjusted his grip on the reins. "What did you say?"

A quizzical look shot across Sarah's face. "Just now? You mean about Lightning being a good horse? He knows what to do. He just needs encouragement from time to time, re-assurance that he is on the proper road."

"Kind of like people."

"Jah."

The sting of angry heat in his chest reduced to the slow burn of conviction.

He knew what he needed to do with this faith he claimed, but could he? Perhaps with some encouragement. The statement Sarah had made seemed to have some truth about it, but how could it when he didn't seem to know anything, especially what to do next?

Was anything he was thinking making sense? With so many holes, he wasn't sure it was. But one thing he would do on trust, as a blind man stumbling with his hands out.

He would trust God more, and ask His guidance in the future.

EIGHT

Sarah was pleased with John's skill in driving the buggy, and she only took the reins back to guide Lightning through the back parking lot of the Commons Market. She tied the horse to the hitching post at the side of the large, long building and grabbed the dried-apple pie for *Mammi* Mary.

Caution was always wise, but was John overdoing it? They had escaped the night before, but nothing had happened since. Perhaps the bad men had given up their search? *Ach*, did bad men ever give up, though? John had paused as she secured the horse and buggy, looking carefully around the parking lot and the doorway, his face a mask of alertness and care.

Inside, the Commons Market was a bustling business with rows and rows of vendors hawking their wares. Surely, they were safe in there, with so many, many people milling about. She had been in the market on many occasions, looking for a friend and completely unable to find her in the crowd. They could disappear in here without difficulty.

John let the door close slowly behind him as his eyes grew wide. "Is it always this busy?"

"No. Sometimes, it is busier." She pointed to a vacant table. "See? Some vendor booths are empty in the winter. In the summer, we sell fresh produce from our gardens. Some sell fresh flowers, both in pots and in arrangements. But now, it is mostly preserves we put up back in the fall."

"Amish goods just taste better than those from the grocery store?"

Heat crept into her cheeks. "That is not for me to say. But *Englischers* tend not to stock up, and they are always looking for someplace to go so they can get out of the house. Word gets out, especially now with the internet, so there are tourists as well as the locals."

"How do you know about the internet?"

"I have seen it here. *Englisch* vendors and customers with their little computers. It is not something I would ever want, even if the bishop did allow it. It seems rather intrusive. Too controlling of their time." She led him through an aisle past a couple of vendors, and then turned right down another long aisle.

"It looks like you could find anything you wanted in here. From this spot, I see sewing materials, big barrels of candy, clothing, furniture, knickknacks that look handmade, spices. There's even a guy over there selling sandwiches."

"*Jah*, it can be overwhelming."

He stood for a moment, looking around, probably surveying for any threatening people but also trying to take it all in. Considering the quiet of the Amish life he had been living for the past few days, it perhaps seemed like a lot of noise all at once. Market days were interesting because they were different, but they were often also too much for Sarah, requiring a strong cup of chamomile tea and an oatmeal cookie in the quiet stillness of her home at the end of the day.

"It's so busy, I would think it would be difficult to find someone in here."

"*Jah*, I have had that problem before." It was bolstering to have a man around again to be helpful and look after her, and this man was comforting enough that she gave voice to her worries. "So, you believe we would be hidden in here? Safe inside the crowd?"

"Yes, but let's find Mrs. Miller as quickly as possible. Okay?"

"*Jah*, I would like that." Balancing the pie in one hand, Sarah removed her winter bonnet and straightened her white organza *kapp* as they walked down the long aisle. She turned to find John staring at her.

He cleared his throat, his cheeks brightening into a light shade of pink. "So, um, not all the vendors here are Amish?" He turned his gaze to the others as they passed by the booths.

"A lot of us are Amish, but some are not. Some dress as Amish just to attract buyers." She motioned a few tables down. "We're almost there."

"That's not right. Doesn't it bother you?"

"What *gut* would come of being bothered? I trust *Gott* to sell my goods when I'm here and to provide for me and Lyddie."

Sarah slowed as she approached a booth on the right filled with jar goods, loaves of bread and berry pies. A weight lifted from her shoulders as she spied the elderly woman in the lavender dress and starched white *kapp* organizing her jars. In the past, whatever had been wrong, *Mammi* Mary had been able to soothe with a kind word or a comforting touch or a hot drink. Sarah prayed that would be the case today, although her problem this time was quite a bit larger than any others she had had.

John's heart ached within him at the notion of having such a peace with life's events as Sarah seemed to have. He yearned for that, but how did one achieve it? Especially with an utter lack of memory? But the chatter and commotion of the market around him wouldn't allow his thoughts to develop that idea any further.

Sarah stopped at the edge of a booth where the elderly Amish woman was setting jars on a shelf with her side turned to them. "*Mammi* Mary," Sarah called softly.

The woman turned slowly and squinted in their direction for a moment. She then raised her hand in greeting, a large smile lighting her wrinkled face.

"*Wilkom*. Come. Come."

John caught the pie as Sarah thrust it at him. He watched *Mammi* Mary open her arms to Sarah, and as Sarah returned the hug, a sudden pain struck his temples. He stared at the elderly woman's face, visually tracing the wrinkles that lined her pale skin, startled at the blue of her eyes, and the instant headache lessened to a dull ache.

Slowly, he approached, looking up and down the aisle. This visit was important to Sarah, and could, perhaps, be important to him. But he didn't want to linger too long. It might increase the chance for their danger to be brought upon this woman.

Sarah turned to retrieve the pie, a wide and beautiful smile lighting her face, and then handed it to Mrs. Miller. "Katie made this pie for you, *Mammi*. Dried apple."

"And you brought it. *Danki* to you both, *liebchen*." She gestured to usher them farther into the booth and away from the crowds. "Lyddie is with Katie this morning?"

"*Jah*. She is helpful with the twins."

"Gut." But as John approached, Mary looked hard at his face, her sharp gaze piercing him. An odd expression lit her features. Curiosity, maybe? But surely she would have had many interactions with the *Englisch*, especially here at the market.

He stepped in closer, behind Sarah. As Mrs. Miller took the pie, she continued to stare at John.

"Ach, I am sorry for my slowness." She gestured Sarah toward a door in between her booth and the neighboring stall. "You know where the vendors' break room is. We can have our visit in there. Let me ask my neigh-

bor to watch my tables, and then we will have introductions."

Sarah led the way into the small room and placed the apple pie on one of two tables. A kitchenette stood against the far wall. It was empty of other vendors and had no other entrances, but seemed secure. A small window was covered with a light calico curtain. He stepped to it quickly and lifted the curtain just enough to peek outside. It looked out onto the parking lot filled with horses and buggies, but not a single person was in sight. He allowed himself to breathe deeply, but the infusion of fresh oxygen did little to calm him.

Following Sarah's lead, John removed his coat and hat and draped them over an empty chair. The door opened, and *Mammi* Mary entered, motioning for them to sit at the table. John chose a chair that faced the door, the hairs on the back of his neck standing upright as Mrs. Miller appraised his Amish clothing and then fixed her stare on his chin, which sported only the shortest of whiskers.

Sarah spoke first, although she seemed rather affected by Mary's stare. "*Mammi* Mary, this is John. He was in a snowmobiling accident near my house, and Lyddie and I are caring for him until he is well." She paused. "Until his memory returns."

John extended his hand but quickly withdrew it as Mary continued to stare at him. "It's a pleasure to meet you, ma'am."

"Call me Mary, as Sarah does." It seemed to be difficult, but she tore her gaze from John and looked back to Sarah. "What do you mean, *until his memory returns*?"

"We are not sure what happened. He had an injury on his head, but it could be the trauma of the accident. He cannot remember anything."

John absently touched the bandage that remained on his forehead and just nodded his agreement.

"Nothing?"

"No, nothing."

Sarah continued. "Both Dr. Jones and Katie said that he looked like you. We hoped you might have some information that could help John remember."

Mary shook her head in sympathy, then stepped toward the kitchenette. "Let me get us some cider." But as she retrieved three mugs from the cupboard, poured cider from a thermos and carried the mugs to the table, she continued to stare at him. "Do you remember your name? Is it really John?"

John sipped his cider. "I don't know what

my real name is. Sarah suggested she call me John."

"Where are you from?"

"I don't know. I would guess somewhere in northern Indiana since that's where I am now. But I suppose I could have traveled here from a great distance, also." He shrugged and took another sip. "That's not helpful, is it?"

Sarah smiled at him, but Mary continued peppering him with questions. "What is your occupation?"

"We found a badge from the Fort Wayne Police Department at the crash site, but I don't know if it's mine or not." Should he tell her that he wasn't sure who on the police force was trustworthy and who wasn't? He looked to Sarah, but she didn't give any sort of indication that he should tell more.

Mary lifted her hand to her mouth, her eyes wide and eyebrows raised. "Is there anything you know about yourself?"

"The only thing I think I know is that I like to work with wood. Or at least I know something about woodworking. I discovered that in Sarah's barn yesterday."

"So, you are not Amish even though you wear Amish clothes? You do not have a beard, and yet you are not shaved."

John looked down at his shirt and fingered

one of the suspenders. "Sarah let me borrow these. I don't think I'm Amish, and yet the Amish don't seem completely foreign to me. I don't know why."

Sarah leaned forward to rest her forearms on the edge of the table. "John got some blood on his clothes, so I let him wear my brother's." She caught his glance and then cut her eyes sideways. What she was saying wasn't untruthful, but neither was it the entire story. She certainly had never indicated just how much danger they were in. But Sarah knew Mary, and he didn't. He would trust her judgment. Perhaps she was protecting her elderly friend.

Of the three mugs of cider, only Mary's remained untouched, yet she stood and excused herself, going to stand at the small sink. John shifted in his chair to see her better from the side. She had raised a wrinkled hand and pressed it to her cheek as she stared at the wall.

"Mammi?" Sarah cast a worried glance at John, then pushed her chair back.

Before she could stand, Mary seemed to wipe an eye, then returned to the table, lowering herself heavily into the chair.

John rubbed his forehead, being careful of the bandage. What was his role here? Should he say something? Comfort in some manner? Perhaps he should just excuse himself to check outside and leave the women alone.

He started to push his chair out, but Sarah grabbed his hand. Apparently, she wanted him to stay.

He settled in his chair again, and she withdrew her hand from his and instead pulled Mary's hands together into both of hers. "*Mammi*, are you feeling all right today? You look as if you are seeing a vision."

Mary sighed. "I am, Sarah. The *gut* doctor and Katie were right to send you to me."

She drew away from Sarah and lifted John's smooth, strong hand in her wrinkled and spotted ones. "I think you are my grandson, Jedidiah."

NINE

"I'm what?"

"You're my grandson. And your name is Jedediah. Jedediah Miller."

John shoved back his chair with a loud scraping sound and ran a hand through his hair. The shocking news propelled him to pace the room. It was ten steps from the table to the edge of the kitchenette. Ten steps back.

A pulsing began in his head, not exactly the pound of a headache, but the tight feeling across his forehead he had come to associate with trying to summon a memory.

His shoe squeaked on the linoleum floor as he spun back to the women who sat at the table, both now staring with wide eyes at him. "Jedediah? That's my name?" It did not feel familiar on his tongue or sound right in his ears. The old woman must be desperate for connection with a family member or seeking attention or…or *ferhoodled*, as Sarah would say. Confused.

"Are you sure, *Mammi* Mary?" Sarah's sweet voice that lilted with the accent of her Pennsylvania German seemed to approach him as if through a tunnel.

"For sure and for certain, Sarah. As sure as I am sitting here."

John stopped midstride, his attention and his thoughts no longer under his control but focused on this woman who said she was his grandmother. "Why do you think so?" It must just be speculation.

"You look exactly like my son. The spitting image, I believe the *Englisch* would say. The last time I saw you in the flesh, you were five years old and in the back seat of the Amish taxi, waving goodbye as your *daed* and *mamm* drove away from their family and their faith." A stray tear wandered down the older woman's cheek.

His feet continued him on the path between the kitchenette and the table. Shouldn't he be glad, thrilled even, to have some answers, finally? In a way, he was. But there were no memories associated with this information. He couldn't remember a father or mother, an Amish upbringing or leaving in a taxi. Maybe if there was some connection to a memory, it would be easier to believe.

"*Mammi*, what else can you tell us about John? About Jedediah?"

One thing did seem sure—he liked the sound of his name, whatever it was, on Sarah's lips.

Another thought pierced him, a thought that ricocheted around his aching skull. Did the man who was after them know his real name? He listened at the door, but all he could hear were the common sounds of a marketplace. He crossed to the window to peer outside, but all was calm there, as well.

Mary finally lifted her mug and sipped her cider. Whether or not John was finding any answers in her revelation, apparently she was discovering some satisfaction.

"Your parents' names are David and Miriam Miller." Mary's voice was calm and soothing. "They left years ago, and I have not seen them since. However—" Mary leaned forward and lowered her voice "—when my daughter-in-law, your mother, Jedediah, mails me notes about my grandson, I keep them in a special place."

"You have letters from my mother?"

Mary sipped again, slowly. "This is my family. I love my son, my daughter-in-law, my grandson. My life has not been the same since they left."

John bent himself into a chair across from the woman who claimed to be his grandmother. "So, I'm Jedediah? And I grew up here?"

"Jah." She spread her arms as if to encompass the countryside. "Indiana. Since you were five years old."

A thought pinged in his brain. "So, is that why bits and pieces of the Amish life seem familiar to me despite the amnesia?"

"Jah, I 'spect so."

"Jedediah, huh?" He tried it a couple more times to see how it felt on his tongue. It wasn't bad, but it wasn't familiar either. "Isn't that an Amish name? Or at least a Biblical name?"

Sarah clasped her hands, a grin reaching across her beautiful face. *"Jah.* That is a good, strong, Biblical name. It is a popular Amish name. It means *beloved of the Lord."*

John pressed the heels of his hands to his temples, a vain attempt to suppress the dull ache and revive more memories. "There's a memory in there somewhere. It's a struggle." He exhaled slowly. "I think I may have been called Jed."

"That is short for Jedediah, *jah*? That would be the shorter, *Englisch*-sounding nickname."

Mary ran a finger over the handle of her mug. "Perhaps your parents gave you that name when they left the Amish church."

"Didn't you say my mother sent you letters? Do you still have them?"

Bolting upright, Mary gasped. "*Ach*, I did. Where is my mind?" As she stood, she paused with a stricken expression and ran a gnarled hand over John's. "I am sorry. It is hard to imagine what you must be struggling with in your loss of memory. Let me get the letters. I hide them in a compartment of my money box since no one gets in there except me. It is my most secret place."

John could barely sip his apple cider before she was back, a small stack of envelopes in her grasp.

The paper of the oldest envelope had yellowed slightly, and the faded postmark reflected a date nearly twenty years earlier. The letter was brief and conveyed the simple message that they had settled and all were well. John held it with the tips of his fingers, but as he studied the meticulous handwriting, it was the same as it had been for the past few days. No memories emerged. Not a single one.

Apparently, he had played baseball, second base, and done well in school. A twelfth birthday party had been a particular delight filled with friends and pizza and bowling. His mother had sent a total of five letters over the years, and he sorted through them, noting the growth and development of a person who Mary had said was him. The tone of each letter was stiff and formal, as if written to a stranger.

The last letter was dated just a few months prior. He stood to pace the room again, reading it carefully. "So, I have no brothers or sisters, and I'm not married? It's just my parents and me?"

"*Jah*. That is what the letters seem to say. Something as momentous as another child or a wedding would have been mentioned, I am sure."

A memory flung itself into his mind, and he staggered backward with the force of it.

He was a police officer. Was that his badge that they had found at the crash site? Fuzziness surrounded the memory, but he was sure he was law enforcement. Was he from Fort Wayne, the city on the badge? The memory receded, and he was left without any idea. The letters didn't contain a return address, and the city and state of the postmark were too faint to read, so that didn't help either.

Another memory, this one stronger, pushed him to drop into a chair. A prickling sensation crawled up his arms and seized his chest. He was in danger. They had found him out, and the only end that would satisfy was his elimination. But who were they?

John forced himself to take several deep, cleansing breaths. Panic wouldn't serve any of them right now. He closed his eyes to try to bring the memory closer to his consciousness. *They* were criminals. But not all. One, at least, was someone who masqueraded as being on the side of good and right.

But who?

He opened his eyes to find Sarah and Mary watching him. Mary's lips moved silently. Could she be praying for him, even then?

"It's just too fuzzy." He shrugged an apology. "I know I'm a police officer, just as we suspected, but I can't remember where or what my last activities were, right before the crash."

Sarah reached a comforting hand to him. "Anything you can remember is helpful."

"It also seems that there is something important coming up soon, but I have no idea what." He swallowed, hesitant to give the next bit of information. But after what they had been through, Sarah was not unaware. "The danger is great."

"*Jah*, we knew that already."

"I just can't remember any more than that. So much is still missing." He squinched his eyes shut again to try to summon up images. Who were the criminals? What was their criminal behavior? And what did it have to do with him?

He pictured the police badge they had found in the snow. *Shield.* The word zinged into his mind. That was what it was more properly called. But he could summon no recollection of wearing a uniform or handling a weapon or even who his colleagues might have been within the department. There was at least one officer who was not completely on the up-and-up. But who? And were there others?

The void engulfed him, a black hole that had swallowed all his memories. He was unable to pull out anything further.

And just like that, his head began to pound, right behind his eyes. He wouldn't be able to remember anything else now.

He grabbed his mug and took another long pull on his cider, but it only soured as it hit his stomach.

"Are you well? Are any more memories returning?" Sarah's gentle voice soothed him more than the cider ever could.

"I feel a headache coming in. And no. No

more memories. I'm a police officer, and I'm in trouble, both from a criminal ring of some sort and from someone or some people within the police department. That's all I can remember." He scrubbed a hand over his face. His glance fell on the clock. "What about the market? *Mammi* Mary needs to return to her booth, and I'm not comfortable staying in one place much longer. We need to change our location."

"Just a few more minutes. I have a question for *Mammi* Mary, John, if you will allow me." A sheepish look graced her face.

He nodded and spoke the question that was probably on both of their minds. "If you're my grandmother, then why am I not Amish?"

Sarah returned the nod. He had asked her question.

"You are short on time, so I will keep this sad story brief." Mary sighed and shifted in her chair, fingering one of the ties that dangled from her prayer *kapp*. "The Lord only blessed me with one child. Your father, David. We were unusual within the Amish community. Amish families typically have lots of children. But I savored every moment with him. As children do, David grew up and met a lovely young Amish woman. Your mother, Miriam. Your *grossdaadi*, your grandfather, and I had known her most of her life and loved her like our own. It was not long after they married, and they welcomed you, their first *bobbeli*. A beautiful baby boy."

Sarah turned to smile at him, and John felt a blush rise to his cheeks. "It sounds like everything was fine then. What happened?"

"When you were four years old, your *mamm* had another baby. A little girl. But as sometimes happens, the *bobbeli* was born with problems. Your father, a good Amish man, hitched up the buggy and went for the telephone to call for help. But help did not come fast enough. The baby died."

A pain rose in his chest, surprising him with a sudden heartache for a sister he never knew. Mary's eyes stared at the door as she seemed to relive those days.

"As soon as the funeral was over, your *daed* packed up your *mamm* and you, and you left in the Amish taxi. He was so bitter over what he thought *Gott* had done to him that he would not speak to us. He just left." Mary ran her hand over the smooth surface of the table, multiple emotions running across her face as she seemed to fight to keep control. "I have not seen him since."

Silence fell over the room, grief enveloping John, although nothing that Mary had said seemed familiar to him. He listened closely for anyone approaching the break room, but there was no one. Now that he had just the slightest bit more information, he needed to be even more vigilant for their safety.

"What about your husband? My grandfather?"

"He died years ago, not long after your father left the Amish community. The doctor said it was a heart attack, but I believe his heart was broken by the loss of his family." Mary passed a hand over her forehead as if trying to wipe away the difficult memories. "Because of David's disdain for the Amish way of life, I do not have much information about you. Like I said, I would assume that if your mother had had any more *bobblin*, she would have written when she sent information about you."

"So, I'm an only child." Not that he could remember any siblings, but a new feeling of loneliness invaded him.

"Can you remember if you were raised with any faith? I have not been able to tell from your mother's few letters what their standing is with the Lord. They left here so bitter and angry that I expect they rejected *Gott* altogether."

"I'm just not sure. I think I believe. It seems

right to me. But clearly, I'm not Amish. Not anymore."

A skim through the letters tantalized him, but it only seemed like he was reading about a stranger. His mind had no recognition of the person in the notes. Memories were there, he knew, but they were just beyond his mental grasp.

Sarah picked up one of the envelopes and studied the careful manuscript.

What he did know, though, were three things. First, he wasn't married according to the letters, but still, he was beginning to care too much for his own comfort about the beautiful Amish woman who, even now, smiled as she looked at the letter. Second, the feeling of danger was real and intense. And third, the sooner he could remember, the sooner this could all be over, and he could return to his life.

The question was, would that be for better or for worse?

His name was Jedediah.

Sarah's heart swelled within her, and she wanted a piece of paper and a pencil to doodle that name in the margins like a silly school girl.

Jedediah was a *gut* name.

But no. She absolutely must stop her thinking from going in that direction. John had just stated an obvious truth.

Clearly, I'm not Amish.

She glanced over at him as he hooked a hand into one side of his suspenders, deep in thought. The green of his shirt complemented the vivid green of his eyes. *Ach*, he was handsome in his Amish clothing. For sure and for certain.

He might look Amish on the outside, but on the inside he was *Englisch*. Raised that way. Living that way. *Jah*, the look on the outside was important to a girl. But just as important, even more so perhaps, was the inside. A man's standing before *Gott*.

His *gut* qualities made for quite a long list. Many qualities her own *daed* and *mamm* would approve of.

"Jedediah Miller." It was a whisper as she examined the envelope.

A warm hand rested on her sleeve. "What is it?"

She looked up into John's eyes, questioning and probing like she had a startled look on her face. She probably did.

Mammi Mary pushed her chair back and stood, the sound of the scraping against the floor breaking the connection with John.

Of course, it was foolish to think that he might consider returning to the Amish. She shouldn't even entertain such a notion. His family had left the Amish church, and he had an important position within the *Englisch* community.

She stood and moved next to *Mammi* Mary at the sink. "Let me wash those mugs, *Mammi*. You probably need to return to your booth."

Mary placed the cups in the sink and stepped toward the door. "*Danki*. I hope I have been helpful. Stop to say goodbye before you leave."

The cold water of the faucet hit her hands as John opened the door for *Mammi* Mary, bringing her back to the present day. Mary said *danki* for holding the door, and Sarah turned back to the sink, refusing to look at John. *Ach*, his Amish clothes looked so natural on him.

But his caution as he opened the door invaded her daydream, a reminder of their danger. Not that she could forget that her life was at stake. Once he remembered who he was and returned to his job in his world, an event that surely would happen soon, he would be gone. Gone back to his police officer job that required the carrying of a weapon and an everyday potential for danger.

And she would probably move, with Lyddie, back to Lancaster County and marry the man her mother had found for her. An Amish, peace-loving, nonviolent man who would never use a gun, except, maybe, to hunt for food to feed his family.

If John was committed to his job that involved violence, then he would never have any interest in becoming Amish. If she was committed to remaining within the Amish church, the only church and community she had ever known, then she would never have any interest in becoming *Englisch*. It was a tangle for them both.

A tangle?

Sarah shook her head to clear her thoughts, the white starched ties of her *kapp* swinging back and forth. There was no tangle. There was simply danger, evidenced by John's hesitation at the door and his careful look outside. When it was over, John—*Jed*—would leave.

It was better that way. Was it not?

With a promise to stop at *Mammi* Mary's booth on their way out, Sarah placed the mugs back in the cupboard and then lifted the curtain on the window just enough to check on Lightning. Dark clouds filled the sky and threatened overhead, and she was grateful that her church district drove enclosed buggies with storm fronts to hold back the wind and snow and keep at least a little of the cold out. It might make the upcoming drive a bit more comfortable.

A shudder coursed through her, but it wasn't anticipation of the cold this time. Gratitude for the enclosed buggy filled her for another reason—safety. She refused to let her mind wander to the targets she and John would be in an open cart.

She turned back to the table to see John— *Jed*—fidgeting with the edge of the pie. Was he nervous about what he had learned? Did it not sit well, his name and occupation?

"Was it a *gut* thing that we came here to see *Mammi* Mary? You know who you are now, *jah*?" Surely to discover one's true identity after a case of amnesia would be a relief.

"Yeah, it was good. But I wouldn't say I know who I am. I have a name and an occupation, but nothing more. And even the name and occupation don't feel familiar or right to me."

"Perhaps in time they will grow more comfortable."

Silence grew between them before John answered. "Maybe."

"What about your *mamm* and *daed*? We could contact them."

"You didn't notice? There were no return addresses on the letters. But I can look for a David and Miriam Miller in Fort Wayne as soon as I have access to a computer." He rose to check out the window, leaning near her to peer out the window from her direction. Was it truly just last night that she had thrown the boiling water in the face of the intruder and then run from her house? It was only a matter of time before he found them. That was the reason for John's caution.

Ach, he was so close. His scent of wood and sawdust tickled her nose. She needed a distraction from him, and fast.

As he pulled away and returned to his seat, she cleared her throat. The last thing she wanted was to sound choked up or emotional over him. "What about your name? Do I call you Jedediah now? Or do you continue with John?"

He looked at her and shook his head as if he couldn't believe he was in a situation that required such a choice. "Neither feel right. But I've become accustomed to *John* over the past couple of days. And it might be safer. Keep me incognito until I can remember more. Assuming the guys who are after us know my real name, I wouldn't want them to hear you call me Jedediah and figure it out. It could put us in further danger."

"But you are in my brother's clothing. That is not disguise enough?"

Her brother's clothing. That's all he was doing, wasn't it? Playing dress-up?

"I don't know if it's disguise enough, but I don't want to take a chance." John glanced at the clock, but he couldn't remember what time they had arrived at the market. "We should move on. We've been here long enough."

A sigh trickled out of Sarah as she lifted the pie from the table and placed it in the refrigerator. "*Jah*. Let us remind *Mammi* Mary of her pie on our way out."

John placed his palms on the table, but as he pushed himself up to standing, his low-grade headache increased. He sank back to his chair, cradling his head in his hands.

The sound of swishing skirts trickled to his ear, and he soon felt a gentle touch on his shoulder.

"Are you remembering something?"

He searched the darkness in his mind, but it was empty. "No, nothing more. But I wish

I could. I have the feeling it would help us tremendously if I could just summon up the details."

"But we know your name and who your parents are. You are a police officer. That is something, *jah*?"

"It's not enough, though. There was another police officer in on the criminal activity, an officer higher in rank than I am. But who? I can't contact my own precinct because I don't know who's dirty and who isn't. I wouldn't even know which police department to contact anyway. The shield was from Fort Wayne, but was it mine? Am I with the Fort Wayne Police Department, or is the other guy? Or are we both?" He sat upright and slapped his knee, the sting matching the angry heat that grew in his chest. "And what's coming up? What event? I just wish I could figure out how it all ties together."

Sarah scooted a fraction of an inch away from him, casting him a sidelong glance.

Defeat made him sag against the chair. His temper had gotten the best of him, and he'd disappointed Sarah. She didn't need to say a word. Her body language spoke volumes to him. Anger was much more *Englisch* than Amish.

"*Gott* will do what is His best will for you." Whether she meant it as an admonition or not, Sarah's quiet statement struck deep to his soul. Was he a believer, as he had speculated? It resonated within him, a yearning to know and praise God. If he was a believer, then God should be taking care of them, right? Certainly, Sarah had just said so. Was He? Was He there, looking at them both?

Look at the evidence. John shifted in the chair. Was that his law-enforcement training kicking in? Or was that the revival of his faith instructing him to count his blessings? It didn't matter where it came from as long as he followed through. He was still alive, even though he could have been killed, apparently a few times over, by now. He had survived the snowmobile crash and the rocks. He had lost his memory and suffered a few scrapes, but he was in safe hands, at least for the moment. He was not in the hands of the bad guys, whoever they were.

So, what next? He was eager for a purpose, a plan that would help him to know and understand where he was going. This indefinitely temporary position in limbo was unnerving at best, maddening at worst. He couldn't traipse about the countryside, hiding from place to place, pretending to be Amish for the foreseeable future, no matter how fetching the Amish woman was beside him.

TEN

Sarah collected her cape and bonnet from the chair. "We have the information we were seeking. Is it time to go?"

John simply nodded and grabbed his coat and hat. He paused at the door and opened it slowly. Sarah stood behind him, stretching to her tiptoes to see over his shoulder.

"It looks clear."

But as John opened the door further, Sarah gasped to see the crowd of customers gathered at *Mammi* Mary's. It seemed that everyone in the market had decided to shop at her booth.

Mammi Mary turned toward her money box and locked gazes with Sarah. A wide smile pushed the wrinkles aside. "Sarah, can you help?"

Sarah pushed gently on John's shoulder to urge him from the break room. "Just for a few minutes, John? The income is so important, and it is a *gut* crowd."

John agreed, and *Mammi* Mary turned back to her customer. Sarah quickly stashed her outer garments under the nearest table and rose to see a familiar face. "*Wilkom*, Mrs. Granger. How may I help you?"

The customer leaned to the right and seemed to make a deliberate point of noticing John, who stood a few steps behind Sarah. "Good afternoon, Sarah. You're here with a gentleman friend, today?" Her bright red lips that matched her bright red blouse curled into a knowing smile, and the earrings that dangled to her shoulders shook their agreement.

Heat leaped into Sarah's cheeks. It was not the first time someone had tried to make a match, and she knew Mrs. Granger's intentions were honorable. But right in front of John? She needed to downplay the situation right fast. "He is helping to carry the boxes today."

"Mmm-hmm. If you say so." The customer prattled on as she picked up jars to examine the labels. "I shared some of the pumpkin butter with my book club last week, and they just went wild. So, I want some more of that. And my Harold loves jalapeño jelly. I could never stomach the spicy stuff, but he just spreads it thick on a cracker and gobbles it down." She laughed at herself, her earrings bobbling with mirth, as well.

"I am glad you like Mrs. Miller's preserves." Sarah darted a look around, suddenly aware of the number of people there. What if their pursuers were hiding in the crowd? She rubbed her hands together to keep them from shaking.

"Last week, and the week before, and the week before, I looked at the chowchow. And I think I'm ready to try it. Do you have any today?"

Sarah turned to look through *Mammi* Mary's jars on the shelf and found John surveying the crowd. The intensity of his vigilance soothed her somewhat. She found two jars of chowchow and forced her mind on the income that *Mammi* Mary so desperately needed.

Mrs. Granger grasped the jar, her red-painted fingernails a contrast to the yellow of the chowchow. "Now, what is in this? Mary told me last week, but I just can't remember."

"It is a pickled relish. Chopped pickles, seasoned mustard, fresh vegetables from the garden." Sarah placed the other jar of chowchow on the table.

"And what do I do with it?" Mrs. Granger

twisted the jar over and around, watching the yellow-orange, thick and gooey substance slosh inside.

"Whatever you want—hamburgers or beans. My little girl likes it on her mashed potatoes."

The customer pressed her lips together as she considered the chowchow. "Okay, I'll try it. And I have these others, as well." She dug around in her sizeable leather purse and brought out two twenty-dollar bills to hand over to Sarah.

Sarah accepted the money and handed it to John, who had appeared at her elbow. "Let me do that." She turned just enough to see that John sported a dazzling smile aimed directly at Mrs. Granger. Had he heard her earlier comment about her gentleman friend? Sarah fisted her skirt, a vain attempt to dry the perspiration that now slicked her palms.

He handed her a paper sack from a pile next to the money box and then turned his attention away.

"He's handsome." Mrs. Granger seemed to be trying to keep her voice low, but it surely wasn't low enough for Sarah's liking. "Will I be seeing him again?"

Sarah gently placed the jars into the bag. All she could manage was a shrug of the shoulders and a glance at the nearest door, longing for a quick exit. The money box creaked open behind her, but where was John with the change?

A touch on the shoulder turned her attention away from Mrs. Granger. "Can you finish this? I'll be back in a minute. Will you be all right here with Mrs. Miller?" John's voice sounded near her ear.

She turned to find John holding the two twenties out to her. His skin had a green tinge, not unlike the color of the money, and he looked rather woozy. "I will be all right. Are you not well?"

He did not answer, just walked toward a nearby vendor.

"John?"

"The flu is going around, Sarah. Maybe he's coming down with it?" Mrs. Granger's comment forced Sarah's attention away from John as he retreated from the booth. "Chicken noodle soup, that's what my mother always prescribed. But you would know that, wouldn't you?" She took up her bag of jar goods. "Harold's waiting in the car for me. Can you believe he prefers to be out there and not in here shopping? Goodbye, dear. See you next week."

As the customer turned toward another

booth, all Sarah wanted was to find John and see what was wrong. She turned in the direction he had gone and found him two vendors over, staring blankly at a quilt, still a little green. But with the money box right there and customers still pressing into *Mammi* Mary's booth, she couldn't chase after him.

Mammi Mary needed her, so she helped another customer, keeping John within view. But as the customer finished and turned to go, Sarah found Sheriff Jaspar approaching, another man with him.

Her throat seized her, a lump forming immediately over which she could not swallow. The sheriff? The man with him was a bit taller and looked to be solid strength, with a swagger in his walk that communicated to Sarah that no one should challenge him.

She cleared her throat, as if she could cough up the lump. Perhaps she should just treat him like a customer? She would give Mrs. Granger her jar goods for free if she could just have her back at the booth, rather than these two.

But as the sheriff stopped directly in front of the table, she found her mouth completely dry and unable to form any words. Why did this man strike such fear into her? Or was it the presence of both of them? Whatever it was, the sooner they stated their business and could be on their way, the better.

"Good afternoon, Sarah." A half smile snaked across his fleshy lips.

A shiver slithered up her spine. All she could manage was a nod.

"This is Simon Carlyle. He's a fellow law-enforcement officer. We're looking for someone who's gone missing."

"Well, Jaspar, don't scare the girl." Carlyle's grin portended maliciousness, and his evil tone felt like a hand closing on Sarah's throat. "We're just looking for someone we haven't heard from in a while." His left eye twitched as he spoke.

Well, this was a whole new level of being *ferhoodled*. For sure and for certain, they were looking for John. Otherwise, why ask her? Her hands took on life and fiddled with the jars on the display shelves while her heart threatened to pound out from underneath her apron.

"The man who was at your house. Did you say he was your brother?" The sheriff rested his hand on the weapon in his holster.

She glanced toward *Mammi* Mary, but she seemed to be deeply involved in helping a customer. It took all her energy, but as much as she wanted to, Sarah did not look around for John. Wherever he was, she prayed he was out of sight. He was not her brother, but if she didn't answer the question, was that lying? "He is no longer there, but I thank you for your concern." She held her breath.

The sheriff didn't speak, just stared, his dark eyes boring into her, as though if he waited long enough she would spill out all the information he sought.

The blackness of his stare threatened to crumple her, even as a muscle around her eye began to spasm. She was desperate for John's return to help her, and yet she didn't want to put him or *Mammi* Mary in harm's way.

What should she do?

The scent of it overwhelmed him, a mixture of ink and paper and a metallic odor that John could nearly taste. A hint of throbbing began at his temple, but this time it was coupled with a wave of nausea.

It was the money. The two twenty-dollar bills that Sarah had handed him. Even after he had given it back and walked away, as far away as he dared with their pursuers possibly lurking nearby, the odor tickled his nose, clinging to him. But why was it affecting him so?

A memory lurked. Its elusiveness irritated

him like a scratchy tag on a new shirt. He couldn't quite reach it, and he knew that if he could just get ahold of it, he could rip it out.

He had stumbled two booths over, far enough away he wouldn't have to answer questions from customers but close enough that he could keep an eye on Sarah. He held his fingers to his nose. The scent lingered on his skin. A tsunami of lightheadedness passed over him, but he powered through it, looking up at the ceiling to steady himself.

The customer with the bright red blouse had left not long after John, and so John had studied the booth around him. He picked up a small wooden sign, stained a deep brown, that had been painted with the phrase Plain & Simple. The wood had been sanded but it was still rough enough to scratch at his hand and pull him away from the agony of a lost memory. A basketful of dolls in Amish dress but without faces rested nearby. Snowmen made with socks and colorful buttons filled another basket.

John surveyed the booth and the area beyond it as the booth's operator helped a customer with an armful of purchases. The operator accepted the bills from the customer, and John felt fixated on the stack of ten-dollar bills in her cash box. That memory, whatever it was, hovered near the edge of his mind, tantalizing in its closeness yet completely out of his reach.

If he closed his eyes, would that help? If he blocked out all distractions and tried to summon one single image connected with the odor of the ink and paper of the money, could he remember? Would his mind be able to connect the dots as to why the aromas brought such strong sensations?

He lowered his eyelids, letting the darkness consume him. The noise of the market around him still filtered through, but with effort he could ignore it. The vivid green of a twenty-dollar bill floated in the blackness, but nothing else. Maybe it had nothing to do with the men who were after him and Sarah. Maybe he was a rich man with the love of money. Or perhaps he was a poor man, constantly in need. Either of those were valid reasons for the effect the bills had on him.

There was no point in pursuing that memory any further. He opened his eyes and turned back to Mrs. Miller's booth, rolling his shoulders as if that could shrug off the disappointment that he couldn't remember anything exact.

But the two men with Sarah weren't customers. When had they arrived? John immediately recognized the sheriff and pushed him to the periphery of his concentration. The other man, though…

A jolt like a stroke of lightning coursed through John, and he nearly staggered from the weight of it. He knew that man.

On instinct, he sidestepped to a position behind a rack of handmade signs. He picked one up and fingered it, hoping he looked like he was admiring the merchandise. At eye level there was a break in between the racks of signs, and John peeked through at the two men. The man with the sheriff was definitely familiar. John knew him from somewhere, that much was certain. But no name or place or relationship came to mind. The clothing was nondescript, dark pants with a black jacket, and his haircut and features, from what John could see, were also unremarkable.

Given that he was with the sheriff and that the sheriff had already proven to be less than helpful, John doubted there was any virtue in his visit to Sarah's booth. But as he stared, the all-too-familiar haze invaded his synapses. Just like with the money, though, no memory would come forth.

He jerked his attention to Sarah. The two men pressed against the table, as close as they could get to her. She stood still, seeming to hold her own against the presence of the men. But the way her hands pressed flat against her apron and skirt, the stretch of the skin around her eyes, the tautness of her shoulders… He needed to get back to her and get her away from the men.

Mrs. Miller was helping a customer at the far end of her stall and didn't seem to have seen the sheriff. Still, though, he needed to protect the elderly woman and draw the men away from her. There was one predictable thing about bad men—they were unpredictably bad.

He returned the wooden sign to the rack and pulled his hat farther down on his head. His short buzz cut was nothing like the Amish bowl style of haircut, and the more the hat hid that fact, the better. One step out of the booth made him feel exposed, but the beautiful Amish woman and her surrogate grandmother needed him. He would not fail them.

As he stepped closer, he could hear their voices and see the man's left eye twitching as he talked. A memory pressed on his temples. The man was lying to Sarah. That was his tell, when his eye twitched. John still couldn't place him or remember his name, but perhaps that would come in time.

For now, his mission was clear. Save Sarah. Draw the men away from *Mammi* Mary.

He continued back toward the booth slowly, acting like he was looking at the goods for sale on the way. She glanced at him but managed to keep recognition out of her gaze.

With another pull on his hat, he picked up a jar of apple butter and pretended to examine it. Now that he was close enough to hear, he knew that the two men were pressing her for information about the man who was at her house the other day. About him. One leaned in close with a veiled threat, his hand holding tight her forearm.

With what must be muscle memory, his chest tightened, his arms tensed. Was he ready for a fight? Had he been a brawling man? He pushed those questions from his mind and focused on Sarah, who had edged in his direction.

He replaced the apple butter on the shelf and picked up the chowchow. His disguise as an Amish man was only good as long as it lasted. With his best attempt at a Pennsylvania German accent, he asked Sarah about the goods. "Please, what do you put in the chowchow?"

Relief wobbled onto her face as she looked at him. She looked back at the sheriff with a glance and jerked her arm out of his grasp. "Excuse me, Sheriff Jaspar. I need to help this customer."

Without waiting for him to reply, she turned to John. "Each batch is different, *jah*?" She pointed to the jar label, and he prayed that the two men didn't notice the slight wobble in her hand. "This has green tomatoes, some red and yellow bell peppers, cucumbers and onion. Also some carrots and green beans from the garden."

"Sounds *gut*." John scruffed a hand over his chin. He didn't have the beard of a married Amish man, so perhaps he could pass himself off as unmarried? But he did have a few days of stubble, and he had no idea if an Amish man ever had stubble.

As he slowly placed the jar on the edge of the table, he snuck a glance at the man with Sheriff Jaspar. The man was staring at him, fine wrinkles on his forehead creased in recognition. For a moment, their eyes met, and John struggled not to step back from the cold deadness in the man's eyes.

"Jedediah," the man hissed. He snaked a hand out to grasp John's arm.

Forcing himself away from the man's stare, John glanced at Sarah with a small nod. "*Jah*, I will take this." But instead of picking up the jar of chowchow again, he let his free hand knock it off the table along with a couple of jars of canned tomatoes. As the containers fell, he jerked his arm out of the other man's grasp.

The jars shattered as they hit the floor. The many ingredients of the chowchow mingled with the tomatoes to form a sticky, red-and-yellow mess that spread quickly across the cement. The two men jumped back to protect themselves from the bits of glass and goo as a large splotch hit John's leg. The man who had just grabbed John slipped on the edge of the mess, flailing his arms out to steady himself.

"*Ach*, I am sorry," John called loudly as he stepped back. "What a mess!" At his exclamation, a couple of other Amish and a few nearby customers and vendors noticed the spill and rushed to help clean it up. One vendor grabbed a roll of paper towels nearby and inserted himself in between John and the men, ready to drop to his knees and wipe it up.

It was just the muddle he had hoped to create. Well-intentioned folks muscled in to help with the cleanup, brooms appearing to sweep up the glass that had scattered even to other booths. John hated to cause the mess for others to clean up and waste Mrs. Miller's jar goods, but it provided a way out. He dashed around the table and grabbed Sarah's hand, heading for a door marked Exit. At the door, he glanced back at *Mammi* Mary. She nodded at him, an acknowledgment of gratitude for what he had done to draw the men away, and held her hands together as if praying.

Inside the door, though, a hallway appeared before them, but it was better than back to the booth. "Come on," he urged her, and then maneuvered them down the hallway toward a corner. Crates and boxes and folding chairs littered the area.

Halfway down the hallway, Sarah's hand slipped out of his as he rushed on. "Wait!" Her cry of help turned him back to find her skirt hem snagged on a stack of crates. "I am caught." She sought the spot of fabric that had stuck on the wooden edge and tugged, but it remained fast.

"Do I bring the crate?"

"No. It'll slow us down. Let me help." He bent over the offending stack of crates, alternating between frantically trying to loose the material of her skirt that was caught and looking back the way they had come. No matter which way he worked it or how Sarah twisted it, the fabric would not come free.

"Look." Sarah's whisper was laced with panic.

The sheriff and the other man stood at the end of the hallway, the direction from which John and Sarah had come.

They were cut off. Whatever lay around that corner, that was their lot.

With a loud rip, John tore the skirt loose.

Free again, Sarah dashed down the hallway. John followed close behind, spurred on faster as the sound of the men's shoes clumping on the floor seemed to catch up with them.

Around the corner, a door loomed up. John nearly bumped into Sarah as she grabbed for the handle. "Out?"

"Yes. Go!" He reached around her to grab the door and laid a hand on her back to propel her outside. The blast of cold on the perspiration that dotted his face made him gasp, but he gulped in a large breath of fresh air and pushed on.

He quickly assessed that they had come out the side of the building. Pointing the way, he followed Sarah around the closest corner and to the back of the brick building. Just ahead of them, a row of tall arborvitae trees formed a hedge around a Dumpster.

"There." He kept his voice low, but a glance back showed the men had not caught up. "Behind the evergreens."

The stench hit him as soon as he found secure positions for both Sarah and himself. His stomach roiled at the stink of rotting food and whatever else had been placed in the large garbage bin. He prayed they would not have to hide there for long.

A small break in between the trees afforded a protected view of a portion of the parking lot. John leaned forward, the scratch of the evergreen limbs scraping on his face. The sheriff's vehicle pulled into view, and John jerked back, pulling a branch across him. Through the needles, he watched the car cruise by, the sheriff at the wheel and the other man in the passenger seat. They were scanning both sides of the parking lot, but as far as John could tell, they didn't have any idea where he and Sarah had gone.

John slowly pulled the hat farther down over his head and forced himself to return slowly to his spot deep in the arborvitaes. Sarah was watching him with wide eyes, and he put his finger to his lips to signal her to remain quiet.

She was trembling, and he took her hand to steady her as he motioned for her to get down behind the Dumpster. One side of their hiding space was completely open to allow access to the garbage bin.

As he lowered himself to his knees, the sheriff's vehicle stopped, directly in front of their hideout.

ELEVEN

John steadied himself against the bin, his heart twisting within his chest at the sight of Sarah. Her lips were blue from the cold, and her hands trembled from fright.

The sheriff and the other man were still there, hovering on the opposite side of the trash bin. The hum of the car's engine buzzed in his ears and pulsed through his arteries.

Running wasn't an option. Even if they could sneak through the evergreens, surely the movement of the branches as they pushed through would alert the men to their presence.

Staying wasn't an option. Even in top physical condition, there was only so long a person could stay squatting on his haunches. Add in the bitter winter cold, and their time was limited.

And now he had to sneeze. The tickle quickly became overwhelming, and he wiggled his nose even though that did nothing to alleviate the irritation.

The vehicle's droning sound began to move away. He hadn't heard a car door, so it seemed safe to assume that both remained in the vehicle that was now leaving. Sarah continued to stare at him, her eyes shadowed with fear, and he cut his view toward the other side of the Dumpster, hoping to communicate with her that he was going to check on the other side. After a gentle reassuring squeeze of her hand, he withdrew from her grasp. On the balls of his feet, he spun toward the edge of the large bin and peered around the edge.

There was nothing there.

He paused, listening intently for the sound of any vehicle. There seemed to be the whine of an engine a way off, perhaps even two. But that could be traffic through the parking lot or from the road on the other side of the building. He stepped from behind the Dumpster, his muscles tensed and ready to flee if necessary.

A few quiet steps took him to the other side of the trash bin and the edge of the building. He exhaled slowly and then peered around the corner.

There it was. The sheriff's car had just reached the other end of the market building and was turning the corner to drive through the front parking lot and, hopefully, to the exit onto the main road and far, far away from Sarah and him.

He ducked behind the corner on the chance that the sheriff might glance that way as he turned. His shoulder bumped something, and he turned to find Sarah standing next to him, her lip quivering.

"I think we're all right." His breath formed a cloud in front of them. "But let's wait another minute."

She nodded and hugged her arms around herself.

"Then let's get to your buggy."

Worry lines crinkled around her eyes. *"Jah."*

John was not a parent, but his heart twisted within his chest as he imagined what Sarah must be feeling, in danger and separated from her only child. He, too, yearned for the sweet presence of the child, a realization that nearly knocked the wind out of him. So far, they were unharmed, but he wanted to check on Lyddie's safety and then move on to a safe place.

Quiet surrounded them, and after another glimpse around the corner showed no vehicles, he ushered Sarah back around the

Dumpster and through the arborvitaes. In a few minutes, they had untied Lightning and were back in the buggy. Sarah grabbed a couple of heavy blankets from the back and settled one around her shoulders, handing the other one to John. He pulled it over his back and around front, grasping it in one hand as he held the reins in the other.

"Perhaps the blankets will make us look different than we did in the market, in case the sheriff drives by again." He gave his *tch-tch* to the horse to urge him forward.

"*Jah*. But what if they do not?" Sarah leaned back, as if to hide farther in the recesses of the buggy.

"We'll handle that if it happens. Could they recognize Lightning and the buggy?" The horse twitched his ears at the sound of his name.

"An Amish person would, for sure and for certain. But probably not an *Englischer*. Would they not pay more attention to cars than to horses? And I do not think the sheriff has been here long enough to become familiar with everyone and their animals."

"Yes, I think you're right." No matter what others might think of the Amish, and he certainly had no recollection of what his impressions had been before he hit his head, Sarah was a very bright and perceptive woman. Yes, she would be considered old-fashioned. Yes, they chose to live differently from the rest of the world. But that didn't mean they were any less intelligent. If anything, her slower pace of life had probably served her well and made her notice much more.

As they drove away from the market, Sarah took back the reins.

"Is there a different way we can return to Katie's house? Just to be safe?"

"*Jah*. But it will take a little longer."

"That's fine. I think that would be the safer course of action."

John was relieved to give up the control of the horse to the person who knew better what to do. Driving an animal to pull a buggy was something that took more skill than he seemed to have at the moment. He peered out the small window and strained his ears for any cars approaching, but the couple of vehicles they did encounter just passed slowly.

"Who was with the sheriff? Did you catch his name?"

"*Jah*. The sheriff introduced him as Simon Carlyle." She glanced at him as if expecting a reaction.

John tumbled the name about in his mind. Were there any connections? He shook his head. "It sounds familiar, like so many other things, but I just can't place it. And I didn't recognize his face. What else did the sheriff say?"

"They said they were looking for someone they had not seen in a while and asked about the man who had been at my house."

"Me." The sour taste of bile coursed upward in his throat. "What did you say?"

"I did not lie." Her voice was adamant, but was she trying to convince him or herself? "I said he was no longer there. That is true. You are not at my house. You are here."

He grinned, that feeling of the simple upward curve of his lips bringing a needed sense of relief, howsoever brief. "That was clever thinking. And I agree. You did not lie." He peered out the window and saw nothing, hoping, in vain, to continue that respite from worry. Whether there was another vehicle there or not, he would still worry…until his full memory returned, and he could fulfill whatever obligation he had that was upcoming, an obligation that he hoped and prayed would end the danger for Sarah and for himself. "This Simon Carlyle was not wearing a police uniform, but that doesn't mean that he's not the dirty cop."

"It does not mean, either, that he is."

"And he wasn't the one on the snowmobile, the one who shot at us in the woods near your house?"

"No. I have not seen him before."

"So, we have no more information now than we did before we went to the market."

"We have the name and face of Simon Carlyle. Perhaps that will come to have meaning for you in *Gott*'s time."

It sounded nice to hear from Sarah's lips, but John was beginning to doubt whether he would ever remember anything more.

The return to Katie's house was uneventful, and relief coursed through John at the sight of it. Inside, after a long hug for both Sarah and John, Lyddie returned upstairs to play with the twins, and Sarah filled her friend in on the basics of their trouble at the market.

Katie quickly fixed mugs of hot chocolate and set out a plate of oatmeal cookies. "For warmth and comforting," she said. "And you must not return to your house but stay here. Whoever these men are, they will not know you are here."

"But the sheriff might. If he does not know yet that we are friends, he could find out by just asking around. And then if he brings that trouble here…" Sarah seemed to swallow hard, unable to finish her thought.

"Sarah's right. We can't stay here, but thank you for offering." John glanced toward the stairs, but only giggling trickled down from the second floor. "The danger has now increased since we stayed last night. I don't want to bring that to you or to any of the Amish community."

Sadness shadowed Sarah's eyes. "*Jah*, we must go. We will take Thunder also, behind the buggy, so you do not have the task of caring for another large animal."

Katie placed a hand on Sarah's arm. "You must leave Lyddie here. With me."

Sarah held her breath for a long moment and then exhaled slowly. "It pains me, but I had hoped you would offer."

An odd sensation coursed through John. He would miss Lyddie's smile and blond curls, and yet he knew they had to consider her safety, as well. Plus, it would be easier to stay safe with just the two of them. "*Jah*, it is the right thing."

Sarah smiled at his use of the Pennsylvania German, but as she turned toward the stairs to call for her daughter, he spied her wiping away a tear. Was she trying to hide her concern from Lyddie and the twins so that they weren't scared? Or was she worried about whether she would see her daughter again?

If John wanted to admit the truth to himself, it was probably both.

Lyddie bounded down the stairs as the women stood from the table.

Sarah seemed to paste a smile on her face as she turned to the child. "Lyddie, John and I need to go out, but you are going to stay here with the twins and Katie. I will be back as soon as I can." She pulled Lyddie into her embrace.

"How long will you be gone, *Mamm*?" The child leaned into Sarah, and John felt a tear spring to his own eye.

"I do not know, *liebchen*." Sarah's voice quavered with emotion.

Katie stepped toward the pair and put her hands on Lyddie's waist to pull her around gently. "We will make fresh cookies and bake bread, and you can play more with Ruth and Rebekah. We will have a *gut* time."

Lyddie paused to study Katie and then turned to her mother for one more hug before she ran for the stairs. Sarah dried her eyes with the hem of her apron as Katie packaged up the rest of the oatmeal cookies and handed them to Sarah. "Where will you go?"

"School is not in session, so we will hide in the apartment that is over the school. We will be warm, and there are some dry goods the parents brought during the fall term. The small barn will house Thunder and Lightning, and we will take Snowball. She will help look out for us."

"Before we go…" John let his sentence trail off, to gather his thoughts. He couldn't trust many people with his nearly nonexistent memory, but he knew the faith of these two women was solid. The memories summoned by the attack at the market were tantalizing, the odor of the ink and paper of the money still tickling him. Desperation to involve law enforcement pounded at him, but if he made a blind call without enough of his memories, he could call the wrong person and get them both killed.

"Before we go," he began again, "could you two pray that my memory returns?"

"*Jah*. We have been praying already."

"What is on your mind?" Sarah pulled her cape around herself.

"I'm struggling to remember something important that is coming, and I feel like I need to remember soon. Prayer is always a good idea, right?"

The women gathered close to John and bowed their heads in prayer, asking the Lord for the return of his memory and the safety of them both as they traveled to a hiding spot.

His shoulder nearly touched Sarah's, and he inhaled deeply to replace the odor of money with her sweet smell of cinnamon and apple pie. He had only good memories of her—her beautiful face as he awakened in her guest bedroom, her delicate hands as she handed him the cup of chamomile tea, the dusting of flour on her cheek as she made pie crust— and he cherished those as a drowning man grabs onto a life preserver. She had been kind and caring and generous from the start. If he were not to recover his memories but were forced to start over, those would be pleasant memories to have at the forefront of his new life.

The unison *amen* startled him from his musing.

"Thank you." John pasted a smile on his face, praying it would encourage the women. "Let's go, then."

Sarah and Katie hugged their goodbyes as John stepped ahead to the door and checked the backyard. All was clear as far as he could tell, but he would never let Sarah go first.

After one more hug from her daughter, Sarah touched the reins to Lightning's back and urged him down the lane. John sat beside her, blankets at the ready if the cold became too bitter, the malamute trotting alongside. The winter afternoon sun slanted across the yard, casting long shadows over the road. Winter had always been Sarah's favorite time of year—silent snowfalls, sledding, hot mugs of cocoa, warm mittens, cozy quilts. But now? With this danger? A few brown leaves leftover from autumn skittered across the road, startling her and making her look in both directions, as she half expected a bad man to jump out and accost them.

She cut her eyes at the man who sat next to her, the police officer who couldn't even remember his name. He sat tall and strong, keeping vigil over the countryside in all directions. *Jah*, she felt safe with him, but he was still just a human being against weapons that could kill. For not the first time in her life, gratitude for her peaceful Amish life overwhelmed her.

He turned suddenly and caught her staring at him. His green eyes flashed at her, and she adjusted her grip on the reins to hide the trembling in her hands. At least the shaking in her knees was hidden by her skirt and cape. She broke the contact and turned quickly back to the road.

The feeling of attraction wasn't new to her. The memory of her deceased husband enveloped her, and a yearning for that close companionship overwhelmed her. Some days—many days—she felt completely and utterly alone. But her husband had been Amish, and their union was sanctioned by the holy Word of *Gott* and by the Amish church. A relationship with this man beside her could not happen, not without leaving the Amish church, something she was not willing to do.

"What is this apartment like?" The low rumble of his voice sent a shiver down her spine, and she used her free hand to rub her arm, hoping to pass it off as a chill from the cold.

"It is small with only two bedrooms, fit into the attic space of the school building."

"And it's for you since you're the teacher?"

"*Jah*. Because of the amount of land available here in northern Indiana, unlike in Pennsylvania where it is quite crowded, the Amish farms and families are more spread out. Sometimes, a teacher has to travel quite a distance to get to the schoolhouse. Especially for the younger girls, the ones who are not yet married, it is too far to travel every day, back and forth to their family's home. So, the teacher could live in the apartment during the week and then go home to family on the weekend. Also, we will not pass it on our route, but there is a very busy road with only a yellow blinking light at the intersection that most have to cross. It is dangerous in a horse and buggy."

"Are most teachers unmarried?" He shifted in his seat as he turned to check out the back window, and Sarah caught a whiff of his masculine aroma of fresh-cut wood and the wool of his Amish coat.

She swallowed down the dryness in her throat. "*Jah*, I am unusual. But our church district was kind and generous and gave me the position after my husband died so I could provide for Lyddie. I wanted to stay in the house I lived in with my husband. His death was enough to handle already. I did not want that abrupt change of moving to the schoolhouse apartment. And I wanted a more normal home life for my daughter. So, I stayed in our house, and I manage the traffic every day we have school."

As Lightning pulled them over a small rise in the road, the white clapboard schoolhouse came into view. With the exception of only a small barn to the back and side, it stood alone on a large parcel of land. A fence ran along the edge of a tree line, the bare branches scratching and clawing at each other in the wind.

"Is that the school?"

"Jah."

John seemed to study the scene, his fingers scratching across his stubble that was quickly becoming a beard. But only married Amish men wore beards. If they weren't careful, the Amish neighbors might believe him to be a married man, and that would not do for Sarah to ride about with a married man.

"I don't see tracks in the snow, other than what appear to be from animals. I can tell better when we get closer, but at this distance, they appear to have their typical irregular patterns. Of course, Carlyle—you said that was his name, the man from the market?— wouldn't have any reason to come to a closed-up Amish schoolhouse."

Sarah nodded and, a few moments later, got Lightning and Thunder comfortable in the barn. There was very little space for the buggy, so she and John maneuvered it to the back side of the barn. Hopefully, it would be hidden from the road there. She was just grateful that her horses would have warmth and shelter.

She led the way to the back door of the schoolhouse, keeping Snowball close by her side. John followed, using a branch with a few leaves left to try to smooth over their tracks in the snow. The sky was heavy with dark clouds, but that did not always portend a snowstorm.

As they entered the cloakroom, the school-room with the empty desks and the cold woodstove visible through the doorway, John turned questioning eyes to her. "When does school start?"

"Soon." Sarah instructed Snowball to stay close outside as she closed the door and then removed her bonnet and hung it up. A scarf and a pair of mittens hung on a hook, proba-bly left by a pupil, and one child's lone lunch box rested on the shelf above the hooks.

John stepped close behind her and peered over her shoulder into a small room adjacent to the cloakroom. "What's in there?"

"All the rooms are connected on the first level. That is our recess room, where we keep our equipment for the children to play with outside. Baseball is very popular with the boys, so we have a number of balls and bats. The girls like to jump rope. A few other things."

She led him through the schoolroom and to the stairs at the side of the building. Up-stairs, the entire apartment was visible from the landing. "There are two bedrooms because sometimes there are two or three teachers, depending on the number of students."

John quickly claimed the bedroom closest to the stairs. "To better protect us," he said.

Sarah stepped into the other bedroom. It was comfortably sparse and plain, just like home, and the only wall decorations were a calendar with the wrong month and a clock whose batteries must have died.

Gott, protect us here and keep us from that fate.

But the little space was warmed with colorful quilts draped snugly over the beds and, in the main area, a handsome solid-wood table with four chairs. Sarah placed her small bag on the chair next to the bed and returned to the kitchen. Even though it was still midday, the heavy cloud cover created shadows that slanted across the walls, but it only took a moment to light the kerosene lamp.

In the cupboard, she spied some canned goods and dishes stacked neatly. From the back, she retrieved a couple of quart-size jars of vegetable soup. If she remembered correctly, this soup had been given by a student's mother, a woman who was renowned throughout the church district for her flavorful blends of vegetables and stock and spices. Sarah felt a smile stretch across her face as she found a box of crackers and a jar of peach slices. They would eat well tonight, and nothing could comfort so well as a bowl of steamy, delicious soup.

Nothing except the warm embrace of a strong, protective man.

Ach, she was as bad as a youth in her *rumspringa*. And the only running around she was doing now was to stay away from a couple of evil men who seemed to want John dead.

She shook her head as if that could clear her thoughts and focused her attention on lighting the propane-powered stove. It wouldn't take long to heat the soup, and she pulled a couple of bowls from the cupboard and turned to set the table.

But John had returned from his room and stood so closely behind her that she bumped into his chest, her voice stuck in her throat. She wobbled, and he caught her by the upper arms, his face perilously close to hers. So close that she could see the various tints of green in his eyes.

He stood for a moment, holding her arms. Could he hear the pounding of her heart or see the longing in her eyes? Having once experienced love, it was difficult to be alone again, especially in her care of her daughter.

Here he stood, looking so Amish and handsome in his plain clothing...

"Do you think it's cold in here?"

John's deep voice broke the moment, and Sarah stepped back, the cold seeping in between them as he loosed his grip on her arms.

"*Jah*, it is." Sarah hugged herself and rubbed her upper arms where John's warm hands had been but a moment ago, but the sensation of his touch would not leave her.

John took a couple of steps toward the door, a look Sarah couldn't quite identify on his face. Was he embarrassed? Or was he disappointed that he had interrupted their connection with his question? "I'll light the heating stove I saw downstairs." His voice was rough and felt like sandpaper over her. "There's no telling if anyone will notice smoke out of the chimney, but there's no reason for those men to think that we're here, at the schoolhouse. Besides, I don't think we have a choice. We have to stay warm."

"*Danki*, John. You probably saw the woodpile by the barn. There should be plenty. The parents of the students keep it supplied." She forced herself to look away from his intense green eyes and hugged her arms around herself.

He glanced out the window. "The clouds

are heavy, but there's still light to see. But it's overcast enough I should be hidden in my black coat. Be back in a minute."

As she listened to his boots clunk down the stairs and through to the cloakroom, Sarah turned back to the stove. By the time he returned, she had the table set and the meal spread.

As heat began to radiate through the floor, Sarah led them in bowing their heads for the silent prayer. The soup was as delicious as Sarah had predicted, matching the aroma of vegetables and spices that had filled the little kitchen as it heated. But with each spoonful, John ate more slowly. Soon, he laid down his spoon and began to rub his temples.

"What is it? Are you getting another headache?"

"Yes, and they seem to come when a memory surfaces."

"That is *gut*, *jah*? What is the memory?"

"So far, it hasn't been that good. My memories are so incomplete. All I can come up with right now is an image of a woman in a kitchen. I would guess she's my mother, but it's so elusive." He took another sip of soup and held it in his mouth before swallowing. "I think the flavor of the soup is resurrecting it. I don't remember what she looks like. Her face is too fuzzy. There's a feeling of comfort. But…" His voice trailed off as if he was afraid to delve any deeper.

"But what?"

"I feel uneasy when that picture pops into my mind. If she is my mother, then what is there, in that relationship, that troubles me?"

Sarah dabbed a napkin to her lips as she thought. A difficult relationship with one's mother could cause all sorts of heartache. If these were going to be John's memories, maybe he was better off not remembering.

Ach, that could not be. His ability to remember was the only thing that would end this time of hiding and fright.

"You were raised Amish for a few years, but then your parents left the faith. But you also have said that you think you are a believer. Perhaps your unease is because you love your mother, but she is not a believer any longer?"

He rewarded her with a slight smile as he retrieved his spoon. "Maybe you should have been a psychologist."

Heat leaped up her neck and into her cheeks, but was it because of the smile or the compliment? "No. It is just common sense."

"Well, I'm disappointed that I can't remember more."

She grabbed her bowl and glass to carry to the sink. As she turned her back to John, she blinked to hold back a sudden tear that threatened. Of course, she wanted the danger to end, and it seemed that that could only be accomplished by John's memory returning. But then John would leave. He would go back to his home, wherever that was, and his life, whatever it had been.

And whatever his life had been, it certainly didn't include the Amish or her. Not anymore.

TWELVE

The sun was struggling to break free of the heavy, late-afternoon clouds as Sarah retrieved a quilt from the bedroom. An Amish doll, probably one belonging to a student, rested on the top of the bureau. Sarah choked back the tears that threatened, resolving, not for the first time in her life, to be content with the will of *Gott*. John had said a tender goodbye to Lyddie earlier, a look on his face Sarah couldn't quite decipher. Whether or not *Gott*'s will included John in her life and in Lyddie's life, or even whether it included life at all, she would accept it.

Sarah's breath hitched in her throat. Could they be a family? Lyddie had commented about other girls' fathers and understood, as clearly as a six-year-old could, what had happened to her daddy. But what could Sarah do about it? Right now, Sarah was simply grateful that Lyddie was safe.

A noise thumped from downstairs. Her heart raced momentarily until her mind caught up. John had gone down to the first floor to check on the wood supply for the heating stove. He must be stockpiling logs nearby to get them through the night and the next day. As the wind howled around the outside of the structure, a strong gust slammed into the outer wall, and the entire building seemed to shiver.

Sarah pulled the quilt over her shoulders, as much for comfort as for warmth, and returned to the main room to sit at a wooden secretary that stood in the corner. The drawer held ample paper and envelopes as well as her choice of writing utensils. She selected a single piece of paper and her favorite style of pen and settled in to compose a letter that demanded to be written. That did not make it any more appealing or acceptable, though.

The pen scratched across the paper, and Sarah was glad, again, not to have a telephone. *Jah*, there were times the device was helpful. But in the *Englisch* world, she would pick up the telephone and talk to her mother. And right now, she simply did not need to hear her *mamm* babble on about the virtues of the Amish man back in Lancaster County she had chosen for Sarah. The only man in her thoughts was the man downstairs, caring for her by providing warmth.

She forced herself back to the letter and continued.

Dear Mamm,
Lyddie and I are well, and I pray that you and Daed are, as well.

I have prayed over your last letter and your suggestion, and Lyddie and I will return to Lancaster County as soon as I can finalize the travel plans.

She had no idea what this Amish man in Pennsylvania looked like now or what he would do to provide for a family, but her mother would surely fill in all the details if Sarah asked.

But she didn't want to ask. She wanted John, the man she couldn't have. To join the Amish church, John would have to give up electricity, telephones and technology. Could he? Or did he not even remember those things? Could he also give up his weapons? Surely, he had many as a law-enforcement officer. Once his full memory returned, would he not want to return to his former life? Doubt flurried over Sarah like a blizzard.

A step sounded behind her, and a floorboard creaked. She turned suddenly, knocking the paper off the desk.

It was John. She had been so engrossed in her thoughts that she did not hear him climb the stairs. The paper rested on the floor, her writing face up. The last thing she needed was to explain that letter to John. She leaned to scoop it up.

"Everything all right?" He rested a hand on the back of her chair.

"*Jah*. Just startled." She folded the letter and tucked it in her apron pocket. "Would you like a cup of tea? To warm up?"

"Sure."

As soon as the tea steeped, they sat at the table, stirring honey into the chamomile-and-black-tea blend.

"I was looking around downstairs, and I counted twenty desks. Do you have that many students?"

"It varies each year, of course. But at the last term, *jah*. Every desk was filled." Sarah swallowed a sip of her tea.

"And what sort of a teacher are you? Are you one of those stern, pinch-faced kinds?" He crossed his arms over his chest and seemed to pull his eyes and mouth together until he was mimicking a harsh frown.

"No. Definitely not." Sarah couldn't help but smile.

"You're a good teacher, then. One who is understanding and helpful. Fun, even, who reads aloud and does crafts and even plays baseball with the boys at recess." He stood and pantomimed swinging a bat and then lifting his skirts and running the bases around the kitchen.

At the sight of him, Sarah laughed out loud, but immediately placed her hand over her mouth. Too much noise might alert someone to their presence. But John's antics brought a lightness to her heart that she hadn't felt since Lyddie had come running out of the woods to tell her a man was hurt. No, even before that. It was a lightness she had not had since news had reached her of her husband's buggy accident.

John returned to his seat and hooked a thumb in his suspenders. His smile slowly faded as he studied her. "How long will you teach? Until a strong and handsome Amish man comes along and sweeps you off your feet?"

The filmy bubble of her happiness popped. It was all a charade, him in the Amish clothing and learning to drive the buggy and taking care of her, just as much as his running the imaginary bases was a charade.

She must have had a sad or upset look on her face, for John seemed to realize what he had said just a split second after Sarah did. She shifted in her chair, and the letter, through the apron, poked her in the leg, a sharp reminder of the plans for her future that did not include John.

Her last two sips were gulped down. She collected the tea cups, not looking to see if John had even finished his, and washed them quickly, setting them on a towel to air dry.

"Would it be all right if I lay down for a few minutes? For a quick nap?" Her voice felt like a mere whisper, but she beat a hasty retreat toward the bedroom. Just before she closed the door, she spied John staring at his hands and what seemed to be profound sadness etched on his face.

A gray gloominess penetrated his eyelids. Images came and went, and a chill felt seeped through to his bones. Grogginess lay heavy over him like an Amish quilt, but John forced his eyes open. He was sitting in a wooden chair, his chin touching his chest, his arms crossed over his middle. But, where was he? He cut his eyes to the walls, but they were plain and white. He rubbed his arms and inhaled the lingering scent of vegetable soup.

Now he remembered, a prickling sensation that poked about in his mind. He had come to the Amish schoolhouse with the pretty Amish schoolteacher just that afternoon.

He jerked upright. How could he have fallen asleep with danger all around? It hadn't been that long since their escape from the market that morning, and although, in theory, they were hiding someplace no one should be able to find them, he didn't know what resources their pursuers had to be able to locate people. He stood hastily, grabbing the back of the chair before it could fall backward. A hurried glance through all the upstairs windows revealed only the snow-covered countryside. Judging by the late-afternoon light, he couldn't have been asleep more than a half hour. At the door to Sarah's bedroom, he knocked softly. He hated to wake her, but he felt an irrepressible need to know she was still in there, safe.

Quiet footsteps sounded to the door. It opened slightly to reveal Sarah without her *kapp*, her hair slightly mussed.

Sarah was beautiful. That much was for sure and for certain. And she was having a most positive effect on him. She embodied gracefulness and delicacy even as she sipped a cup of coffee, straightened her prayer *kapp* or dabbed at her daughter's mouth with a napkin.

"Is everything all right?" Sarah's eyes were wide with concern.

John shook himself out of his few memories. He needed to concentrate on the here and now. "Just wanted to make sure everything was okay in there."

"*Jah.* I will be out in a minute." She closed the door, and John spun to lean heavily against the doorjamb.

Was he falling in love with her? With Lyddie? Both were valid questions and ones he wasn't sure he could answer. What did love feel like? With nearly all his memories gone and his own given name, *Jedediah Miller*, sounding so foreign on his tongue, how could he know what true love was? The image of her laughing and smiling at his antics earlier filled his mind's eye. That was a memory he would hold on to for the rest of his life. He wanted to stay with her, to continue to get to know her, to soak up her zest for life and love. Yet, could he give up the modern world and join the Amish? Could he be a proper *daed* to Lyddie? If so, it would have to be for the love of Sarah, Lyddie and *Gott*.

As Sarah emerged from the bedroom, hair in place and smoothing her skirt, the hum of a car sounded outside. John immediately locked gazes with Sarah as she tossed him a worried look. From the closest window, concealed by the light blue curtain, John spied a four-door sedan approaching the lane for the schoolhouse. It was traveling too fast and slipping in the snow. As he counted the number of people in the car—two—a flash of memory struck him. His knees began to buckle, but he gripped the window ledge to watch until the car passed their lane and drove out of sight.

Sarah grasped his arm and led him to a chair. "You have another headache. Another memory returning." It was a statement, not a question.

How quickly she had come to know him. "Yes."

"What is it? I know that you are eager to know more about your life."

"Assuming it's good." He squeezed his eyes shut, trying to summon something out of the darkness. "I remember driving in a car and following a man, I think that man from the market, as he drove to an old warehouse. He was driving that same style of car as we just saw outside."

Sarah brought a glass of water and placed

it on the table in front of him, her free hand resting briefly on his shoulder. Whether or not she meant it as a calming comfort, it served that purpose. John felt the muscles in his neck relax as Sarah sat down across from him.

"Remember the doctor said your memory could return in bits and pieces. He also said it was a form of post-traumatic stress disorder."

"I do remember that. I just wish I could remember what is so important that's coming soon. That could end all of this hiding." John's fingers flew, without his conscious thought, to his temples. It had become nearly a habit in the past few days, the rubbing of his forehead when he was trying to remember. Another vision flashed in his mind, and he closed his eyes as it flashed like lightning in the darkest night.

A courtroom. He'd been in one before. Many times, in fact. *Do you swear to tell the truth, the whole truth, and nothing but the truth? I do, so help me, God.* A trial was coming. A couple of weeks, and he would need to take the stand. His testimony was crucial evidence.

But about what would he testify?

Another image flashed, the man from the market. Without opening his eyes, he asked

Sarah, "The man at the market said his name was Simon Carlyle? He's the dirty cop." But were there more? He delved deeper, trying to see more of the image. Who was he with? John couldn't remember anyone else.

The snowmobile accident and the man who had returned. The one who had pointed his gun at them. The one who would have killed them all, given the opportunity. The vision in John's mind was as clear as if he was standing there in the snow. The man was called Jimmy the Bruise, and he ran a counterfeiting ring. The odor of the money at the market hit him like a punch in the face, and he felt his hands fist on the table as if prepared to fight back.

But then everything faded.

As suddenly as the images had flashed, they disappeared.

All was black.

He slowly opened his eyes, letting the light in bit by bit, forcing his hands to unclench and rest on the table. Sarah was watching him, but kindness and warmth and understanding radiated from her beautiful brown eyes.

Not yet had every single memory returned. But it was a lot. "It's time to get the right law enforcement involved. Men I can trust." He now knew who to call. But first, he had to get to a telephone, and keep them both safe along the way.

THIRTEEN

As much as she tried to emanate encouragement to John, Sarah struggled to keep her hands from shaking. "The police? You have remembered more, *jah*?"

John had a wild look about his eyes. "Yes. We need to get to a telephone. Where is the closest one?"

"But there is a snowstorm coming." The closest window revealed dark gray clouds hovering near the horizon. "I can tell by the clouds. If we were to get caught out in it…" She didn't finish the sentence, but she didn't need to. He knew exactly what could happen if they were stranded in a blizzard.

"Look. I can't remember all the details yet. But I know that Simon Carlyle, the guy from the market, is a dirty cop. He was extracting payment from a man who goes by the name Jimmy the Bruise in exchange for protection. Jimmy is the man with the birthmark, the head of a counterfeiting ring. He's the one we saw at the snowmobile crash site. I need to testify in a trial coming up soon. And I think I know who to call for help." He stood and grasped her arms. "At the very least, to keep you safe."

John's voice had risen with emotion, and she put a finger to her lips to quiet him.

"What about your friend? Isn't there a phone shanty outside her barn?" He kept his voice low, but an urgency sparked in his eyes.

"Katie? No. That is the opposite direction of home. And I do not want to bring trouble to Katie. She is raising her twins alone, and Lyddie is there. Neither do I want to bring trouble on *Mammi* Mary, but she does not have a phone anyway. And the market is too far away." She returned the glass to the sink. "It is best to head to the neighbor closest to the schoolhouse, a couple of miles down the road. They are out of town, but we can use the telephone in the shanty near his barn. Perhaps the police could find us there?"

"That'll do. How long will it take to get there?"

"Long enough that we should bring the quilts on the beds for warmth. What about our things we brought from my house?"

"Leave them. God willing, we'll come back

to collect them." Urgency tinged his voice. "Right now, let's get moving and get to that phone. This storm that's coming is only going to make it worse."

Had that hasty departure from home only been yesterday? Right now, as she pulled the quilt from the bed, it seemed as if her life had been spent on the run. The idea of home had never been so sweet.

Fat flakes of snow began to flutter down outside the window, but that only drove her on. She rushed past the window again on her way out of the room, and the snow had grown from flurries to a steady fall in just those few seconds. That would make the drive that much more difficult and slow, but what else could they do?

She had no reason not to trust John. If he thought they were in danger staying in the schoolhouse, then who was she to say any different? Better to take her chances out in the snowstorm with John than to risk facing a gun in the schoolhouse.

John hastily folded his quilt but couldn't help but stare for a brief moment out the window. Large snowflakes quickly covered the plowed road. It wouldn't be easy going, but he wasn't sure what else to do. With the responsibility for the lovely Amish woman weighing heavy on his shoulders and a come-and-go memory that he couldn't rely on, his resources were minimal. Instinct, really, was all that he had. That and prayer that God would protect and provide.

All he knew right now was that they needed to get to a telephone as quickly as possible.

Strike that. That wasn't all that he knew. He knew that he shouldn't just think about prayer. He should do it. But surely God would understand if he kept his eyes on the weather outside and his feet in motion to the door.

God, there's a vague inkling somewhere deep in my soul that we used to talk to each other a lot. And now you know me better than I know myself, although that has probably always been the case.

We need protection as we travel through this snowstorm, and I need to be able to reach someone trustworthy when we get to that telephone. Please, put a special protection around Sarah. If anyone gets hurt, let it be me.

Sarah's shoes clacked on the wood floor as she emerged from the bedroom, quilt in hand. Tension radiated from the fine lines around her mouth and eyes, but as she caught his gaze, she forced a smile.

The woman truly was beautiful. Her blue dress with the white apron contrasted against the deep brown of her eyes, and even though she didn't wear any hint of makeup, her smile made his heart beat more urgently.

"*Ach*, John, are you *ferhoodled*?"

He cleared his throat. "Um, no. I'm fine. Ready?"

But at the top of the stairs, a muffled sob sounded behind him. He spun back to her to find anxiety in her eyes and tears on her cheeks.

She had been trying so hard the past few days to keep going and stay strong, and now she looked ready to crumble. John rushed to her and gathered her in his arms. She seemed to melt into him, resting her head on his shoulder. Soon, dampness from her tears soaked through his shirt.

"I am sorry for crying on you, John." She touched his shoulder where it was wet.

His hand, as if on its own, found her hair and pressed her to him. "No, no. It's my fault. I'm sorry I dragged you into this. I…" What if something terrible happened to her? As he held her, it became perfectly clear that he cared for her deeply. Did he even want to go back to whatever life he had had if he couldn't take her with him? Before they headed out into the snow and all that awaited on the other side of the door, should he tell her how he felt? "Sarah, I want you to know that I care for you. A great deal. Do you think—"

Snowball barked from the yard below, jerking his attention to the nearest window.

A dark car drove over the ridge and into view, cutting off his question and, indeed, his very thought. His arms stiffened around Sarah, but he couldn't take his eyes from the vehicle. It was coming fast. Too fast.

The driver seemed to hit the brakes too late and slid through the turn into the lane that led to the schoolhouse. John stepped toward the window, one arm still around Sarah, and peered out at the car. There were two people in the front seat, and the one in the passenger seat was definitely not Amish. He couldn't make out faces, but both seemed to have the scrunched sinister look of someone on a mission. An evil mission. A throbbing began in his temple, and he swallowed hard.

He stole a glance at Sarah and saw what he had expected. Fear. "Do you recognize that vehicle?"

"No."

He squeezed her around the waist, praying it would infuse her with courage. "We need to get out of here. Now."

They ran to the door, but the car had turned into the lane. Their time was running out.

What if they had left just two minutes sooner? Would they be safe now? But how could they have gone any faster? They had grabbed their outer garments as soon as he had remembered who to call.

At least the enclosed staircase on the outside of the building was on the side of the school opposite from the lane. Their exit could be hidden if they got down soon enough. He opened the door to the apartment, and the wind whipped up through the staircase with a ferocity that took his breath away. Snow swirled in his face, but there wasn't time to linger.

Taking two steps at a time, John led them down. The dog continued barking as John paused at the open doorway at the bottom and peered around. The door that led into the schoolhouse stood immediately to his right, but it did not look as if it had been tampered with. He strained to hear the thrum of the car over the brutal wind. It was still running, but the engine didn't have the sound of a vehicle in motion. So far, they were ahead of the men in the car, but not by much.

Hesitation could cost them their lives. But should they make a run for the barn, through the open yard? That would be their escape, with the horse and buggy, although a buggy could never outrun an automobile. Or should they seek shelter inside the schoolhouse? But that could be their trap if there was no way out once they entered.

Before he could decide and act, the trim around the door exploded. Sarah yelped as he stepped back, one arm flung up to protect his face and the other arm out to hold Sarah back behind the shelter of the enclosure.

A shot had been fired, and it had missed him by mere inches.

His decision had been made for him. He jerked the door open, and with his back to the yard, shielding Sarah, he pushed her into the schoolhouse in front of him. The wind slammed the door shut behind them.

"Get down." He squatted, and Sarah followed.

They inched toward the teacher's desk at the far side of the room, although John wasn't sure why he was leading them there. He desperately scanned the room, but he couldn't see anything helpful in the old-fashioned wooden desks with wrought-iron legs, the bookshelf, the colorful artwork on the walls. At least the green shades were pulled on the windows, but there was nothing that would protect them from another bullet.

They were trapped and completely at the mercy of their pursuers, just like the mouse in Sarah's barn that the cat had caught. But would their end be the same as the mouse?

FOURTEEN

Sarah clutched her full skirt in her fist, desperate to keep from stepping on it as they crept through the schoolroom. She threw up a prayer for Snowball. Her barking outside had stopped, but Sarah had no way to know if the dog had been bribed with a treat or harmed in some way.

John halted, a hand up to pause her. He turned first to the left and then to the right, probably to scan for danger that may have followed them into the school.

Tears threatened, but she blinked hard to keep them at bay. She refused to let them win. *Jah*, it was true that self-defense was not the Amish way. But how often did someone committed to the Amish church and the Amish way of life have her life endangered? Some picked at them from time to time, teased them for being old-fashioned. But threatening her life? It was unheard of, at least in the Indiana Amish communities.

She teetered on the heels of her boots and grabbed a fresh fistful of skirt. What was wrong with running away from danger? Nothing that she could tell. It was human instinct, for sure and for certain.

"What now?" Her voice was such a low whisper that she was not sure John had heard her.

But then he turned to her, and the urgency in his green eyes made her forget everything around her. He didn't respond verbally, but he squeezed her free hand, warmth and confidence and security passing from him to her in his look and in his touch.

As difficult as it was, she forced herself to pull away. To look away. Anywhere but at him. The whole situation was quickly becoming—*jah*, had already become—overwhelming, especially since John's profession that he cared for her. Why did the *Englisch* think they had to voice everything on their minds? Perhaps some things were better left unsaid.

The gloom of the schoolroom seemed to swallow them. As the snowstorm outside intensified, a similar gloom stole over her. She had to admit, if only to herself, that she was falling in love with him, despite what wisdom would advise. But she certainly had no intention of telling him. What would that accomplish?

And especially in the midst of this trouble. She had been ejected from her home out of sheer fright. She had been chased at the market, too afraid to go back to the shelter of her friend's house. And now the shot that she had been fearing for days had actually been fired.

Peaceful. That's what her life had been. Her whole life, up until now, had been lived in harmony with her family, her community, her circumstances. It had not been easy when her husband was killed in the buggy accident, but it had not been like this. Overwhelming. Frightening. Unbearable. She wanted to crumple on the ground and give in. Give up.

Was this the valley of the shadow of death? How did the rest of that psalm go? She had learned it as a little child in school, but now she couldn't seem to get her thoughts straight.

Lyddie's voice reciting the psalm rose up in her mind, and she could almost feel her soft little hand pressed on hers, a gentle whisper of a touch.

Jah, she would fear no evil, for *Gott* was with them. Wherever they ran, His rod and His staff would comfort them.

Sarah closed her eyes in quick prayer. Her

daughter needed her mother to guide her, to protect her, to love her. Sarah would not let her down. She would be strong, if only for her daughter, a *wunderbar* blessing from *Gott*.

John wobbled on his heels, drawing her attention. He looked at her expectantly, but she wasn't sure what he wanted except her trust. He had been a hero, even though he was the injured one. He had protected her, guiding and directing their way to keep them from harm.

But now he looked at her with anticipation imprinted on his handsome face. Just as she needed John to stay strong for her, she needed to stay strong for him. No matter what the future may hold for them, they were in this together, at least for now.

Bobbing forward onto his knees, John grasped her upper arms. She startled, but he squeezed her gently, filling her with encouragement. "You know the school and the area better than I do. How can we get out of here and to that telephone? Can we get to Thunder and Lightning and the buggy? Or is there a faster mode of transportation?"

He was still hopeful, still trying, even though he surely knew the answer. "No, there is nothing faster. We only have the horses and the buggy."

"Okay, we'll do our best. What's the fastest way to the barn?" A door slammed from the front of the schoolhouse. John popped up, turning his head toward the sound, and Sarah followed. "Lead us. Go!"

She turned to the back of the room and maneuvered quickly through the desks. Skirting the teacher's desk, a brief memory of calm and quiet school days with eager students flashed in her mind. A door stood behind and to the side, and she dashed through the doorway, pausing just inside to make sure John had followed.

"The recess room?" John looked around at the baseball bats in their wooden storage box, the shelf of softballs, the pegs with jump ropes and a couple of scarves left behind.

Over John's shoulder, she spied the two men she had seen before as they entered the other end of the schoolroom.

"John!" She kept her whisper low. "They are here."

Sarah took a small and careful step toward the exterior door. She didn't dare to look, but she didn't need to. She knew it was too far away to make a dash for it. Too far away to run to the barn to hitch the horse to the buggy. Too far to get away from the gun he was now leveling at them.

Before John could turn, a bullet shot through the schoolroom. It seemed to stop near her, but nothing exploded this time. A softball rolled off the shelf next to her, but all she could hear as it hit the ground was her own screaming.

Sarah's scream sounded muffled in John's ears as he rushed forward to push her out of the doorway. She held a hand over her mouth, her other hand clutched over her chest.

He didn't have time to pick up and examine the softball that had caught the bullet. Something clicked in him, and survival instincts kicked in as he pushed down on Sarah's back, forcing her to lower herself into a crouch. He apparently had been trained as a police officer. Was that where those instincts originated? Whatever it was, he had to get them out of there, although capture seemed imminent with the advantages in weaponry and transportation their pursuers had.

With his touch on her back, or perhaps because she had run out of air, Sarah's screaming had stopped. In the deathly silence, the slow pound of footsteps ricocheted through the schoolroom. John hadn't been able to turn enough to see the shooter's face before they had rushed for cover. But whoever it was, he apparently thought they were trapped. He thought he had plenty of time to find them and finish what he came for.

He was right.

From his hunched position, John eyed the recess room. He had only a few seconds before the shooter came through the door. His gaze darted about the space, and energy surged through him. Could he take the guy? Maybe, but that wasn't the best course of action with Sarah there. The Amish were nonviolent and didn't want to hurt others. That was fine, and he would restrain himself. But that didn't mean he couldn't set up the possibility of a simple accident.

His gaze caught on the bats resting in a wooden box near the door, the handles leaning against the wall.

That would do.

Silently, he pointed Sarah toward the exit, and she huddled near the outer door. Then, he scooped up as many baseball bats as he could fit in his arms.

The thunder of the footfalls pounded more closely. He held his breath and trained his vision on the floor in the doorway. Too soon, and his plan would flop. He would end up with a bullet through him. Too late, and he could encounter the same fate.

A second set of footsteps joined the first. Both were there, just on the other side of the door.

He darted a glance back at Sarah. She stood, wide-eyed, her hand on the doorknob. He nodded at her, and she seemed to visibly calm, filling her lungs with air and then slowly releasing it. Where her confidence in him came from, he had no idea, but he wouldn't let her down now.

A boot toe appeared in the doorway. *Now!* He let loose all the bats, giving them an extra push with his arms. They rolled across the wooden floor, bumping into each other and crashing loudly. One immediately landed on the boot toe, and the toe disappeared back through the door into the schoolroom.

"Back up!" An angry voice sounded from the next room.

"No. Forward." The owner of that command seemed to be the one in front, for the toe of the boot appeared in the doorway again, kicking at the equipment. Bats rolled and clunked across the floor, now ricocheting back toward John and Sarah.

Without a sound, John gestured toward the door and mouthed, "Go!"

She pulled the door open and stepped outside, Snowball running to meet her. Snow immediately swirled in. In three steps, John was right behind her. As he closed the door, he checked over his shoulder. Jimmy the Bruise had come through the door and was slipping on the bats, about to hit the floor, his weapon waving wildly. The other, Carlyle, grasped the door frame, desperate to stay upright.

Without looking, he whispered to Sarah. "Get to the barn."

The two continued into the recess room, wobbling over the rolling baseball bats. Jimmy the Bruise leveled his gun at John. Could he duck out the door in time to escape the bullet?

But then Jimmy fell, his weapon waving wildly. It went off, the bullet screaming toward the ceiling.

John slammed the door shut behind him and took off running, as quickly as the gathering snow would allow, toward the barn. Sarah was only a few steps in front of him, Snowball running alongside.

As John caught up with Sarah, the dog's barking quickly turned to a throaty growl. That could only mean one thing. Carlyle and Jimmy had emerged from the schoolhouse.

"Stop!"

John halted and slowly rotated toward the angry voice. Carlyle had his weapon pointed directly at his heart.

FIFTEEN

John raised his arms, palms out, as he stared down the barrel of the gun. Slowly, he raised his gaze to the man behind it.

Simon Carlyle. The man from the market. The dirty cop.

"Well, Jedediah Miller at last. You're a hard man to find." A sneer snuck across Carlyle's face. "Are you hiding? Or did you get religion? 'Cause you're going to need it after we're done with you."

John didn't answer. In the silence, Sarah cried out next to him.

She recognized someone, and it drew John's glance to the man behind Carlyle. A nasty bruise-like birthmark crawled from his hand, presumably through his coat sleeve, and up to his neck. A jolt of recognition coursed through John. This was the same man from the snowmobile-accident site, the one that Lyddie had told them about. It seemed like a lifetime ago now, standing at the wreck and looking for evidence of his identity. But there was no doubt.

It was Jimmy the Bruise, the counterfeiter, with ink and, soon, blood on his hands if he carried through with his apparent intent to kill them all.

A sudden headache pounded at his temples. He knew by now that meant that more memories were trying to emerge from the haze, but he could only pray that they were memories that would help them get away from these lunatics.

If only he had a snowmobile.

"Stop your yapping, Carlyle, and get it done." Jimmy had stepped up next to Carlyle. "If you don't, I'd be happy to." Jimmy pointed his gun at John, lining him up in a shot that wouldn't miss, not at that close range.

"Not now." Carlyle swung his arm at the bruised man to lower his weapon. "Stop shooting to kill."

Jimmy growled at him but relaxed his arm.

"We've gone over this and over this. If you murder them, execution-style, it could get back to me. And there's no way I'm going to jail for you or with you. We've got to get rid of them in a way that makes it look like an accident. Not just a shooting."

"I don't care." The Bruise released a word that made Sarah cover her ears.

Sarah's movement caused Carlyle to swing his weapon toward her. "Get your hands where I can see them. Amish Boy here may trust you, but I don't."

In his peripheral vision, John saw Sarah raise her palms toward Carlyle. Her lip quivered, but it probably wasn't from the cold. Snow had piled up on their shoulders as they stood listening to their pursuers argue.

"All right, Carlyle, let's get this done. It's no good to draw it out. Just pop 'em."

"No." Carlyle nearly growled at The Bruise. "Look. You may be a criminal worthy of jail, but I am not. I'm an officer of the law, and I plan to continue in this position without even a smudge on my record."

"Like it or not, Carlyle, you're in this now. Do I need to remind you how much you've profited from this alliance? That makes you a criminal, as well. They need to be eliminated or we'll both end up in the clink." The bruise around his neck seemed to darken as John and Sarah stood in the snow, waiting for their fate to be decided.

"And do I need to remind you how we even found them here? You wouldn't be here without my deductive reasoning."

John turned to meet Sarah's gaze and nodded almost imperceptibly as he took a small step back. Could this be their getaway, with their captors arguing? Sarah also took a step back, worry creasing the delicate skin around her eyes, the dog stuck tight by her side.

"Who cares how we got here? We need to get rid of them, or that trial'll be a slam dunk."

"Fine." Carlyle took a step toward Jimmy. "But not this way. Your type may not care about leaving evidence, but I know a few things about crime-scene investigation, and I don't want a bullet left in them or questionable circumstances. Barns burn all the time in the Amish community, right? Wouldn't it be sad if someone got caught inside?" He affected a pouty expression, but it quickly morphed into a malicious smile.

If that was the plan, the sooner they could get away, the better. John took another small step backward, but before Sarah could follow—

"Hey! You're staying right here. Don't move." Carlyle's weapon rose a notch in their direction.

"Simon." An image flashed. John and Simon Carlyle sitting in an unmarked car, talking and waiting. "Are you sure you want to do this?"

Silence reigned as a myriad of emotions seemed to tumble about the cop. Finally, he just shrugged, an air of resignation enveloping him. "So, you found me out."

John nodded. He remained silent, uncertain how much he should say. It wouldn't help their getaway to antagonize him.

"Yeah," Carlyle continued. "It's amazing what information people are willing to cough up for a police officer. Especially since you haven't told anyone of my involvement. I still have a spotless record."

The late winter afternoon was unusually dark, with heavy cloud cover and snow falling fast. But Jimmy jerked toward the road and studied the horizon and then turned back and motioned John and Sarah toward the barn. "There's no time to waste, not with this weather. Get in the barn."

Carlyle stepped close to John and nudged him with the barrel of his weapon. "And don't try any escape. We'll be right here." The odor of his breath, a smell of stale coffee, pushed John toward the barn door. "You're helpless though, anyway, aren't you? You couldn't have made it easier for us, hiding with the Amish. They don't have weapons. There's no fast car to get away in." He nodded toward Sarah. "She doesn't even have a phone to call for help with. Snow's falling. Everyone's staying at home, where the Amish belong. And barns burn all the time. Too bad that accident happened and took two lives." A snicker escaped through his nose.

He caught Sarah's gaze as he turned toward the barn. She stared at him, the wind whipping the tendrils that had escaped her prayer *kapp*, her beautiful brown eyes clouded by fear and worry, her full lower lip still trembling in the cold. He longed to gather her in his arms, warm her, comfort her, keep her safe. She didn't deserve this. She should be sitting by a fire, wrapped in a cozy quilt, sipping hot cider. Not at the mercy of two gunmen. He nodded, the only gesture that might convey to her that he would do his best. That all would be all right, whether they got away or whether they met their Maker.

Another nudge, harder this time, made him stumble a couple of steps. Jimmy the Bruise was beside Sarah, grasping her upper arm in his meaty hand.

"Let's get going. There's no time to waste." Carlyle pressed again. "We're going to wrap this up, once and for all."

* * *

Sobs, desperate to wrench free, filled Sarah's throat, but she choked them down. Slowly, she marched toward the barn.

She eyed the surrounding woods. Could they hide? Or would this snow and cold prevent any escape? The thought of being without her daughter caused more sobs to fill her, but it was better, at least, for Lyddie to have life than death.

Even a life without her mother.

But would an escape attempt mean an immediate end for them? Probably, except John's look had seemed hopeful. Perhaps he had a plan. For now, she would go along. Trusting *Gott* was not always easy, but it was always necessary. She would choose to trust John, as well.

John opened the large barn door and held it for her. As she passed him, she prayed that he would figure a way out, a way to help them, a way to get away. She couldn't help but glance at him, but he was kicking at the snow. She hesitated a fraction of a second, but it was enough to cause him to look at her. His eyes met hers, and she immediately warmed with the care and protection that issued from his expression. Stress projected from him, but she knew from his eyes, the light of the body, that he would even die to keep her safe.

Carlyle grabbed John by the arm and pulled him away from the door. "You come with me to get the buggy. We'll burn it up, too. Don't want to leave you any opportunity for get-away." He nodded to the man with the bruise-like birthmark. "Stay with her." Snowball ran after John.

Sarah trod into the barn, her muscles tense at the presence of the gun constantly pointed in her direction. A panic rose in her throat at the idea of Thunder and Lightning perishing in a fire. She turned toward her captor and faced his weapon. "Please, let the horses go! They have done nothing to you."

"Zip it, lady." The Bruise pushed her farther in with his weapon. "I don't care about no horses. Get in there."

John returned with the buggy and pulled it inside the barn. Sarah met his gaze as he settled the buggy to the side and swallowed down the lump that had taken up residence in her throat in her efforts to choke back the sobs. A few more minutes with him were minutes well spent.

The moment he finished, the one called Carlyle waved his gun again at her, stepping in too close for comfort. "Okay, in with the horses, you two." He ran his hand over the weapon and then pierced her with his hard stare. "See this? Don't even think about trying anything."

As Carlyle moved his hand toward her arm as if he was going to push her, Snowball rushed out from the other side of the horses. She barked and then bared her teeth to growl. The horses stamped their feet, shuffling nervously in the hay.

Carlyle pulled back from Sarah and stepped away from the horses, a look of vicious irritation clouding his face. "You better control that dog, woman. Or I will shoot it."

"Snowball, no!" Sarah put out her hand to stop the dog. The malamute slowed to a stop near Sarah, still rumbling from deep in her chest.

Before she could get a hold on Snowball's collar, the dog advanced toward Carlyle again.

In a blink, Carlyle swung out his leg and kicked the animal solidly in the ribs. Snowball's loud yelp of pain ripped through the silence of the winter afternoon. She dropped to her haunches but continued to growl.

"Snowball!" Sarah cried. She surged toward the dog, her throat tight, but John caught her and held her close.

"Take care of that mutt," Jimmy commanded.

Carlyle stuck out his foot toward the dog, and Snowball crouched again. Getting behind her, Carlyle chased the dog behind the barn. A moment later, he emerged alone.

Sarah swallowed hard. But other than soak up John's comfort, there was nothing she could do. To antagonize these men any further was a certain death sentence. With that thought, her strong facade crumbled. She could no longer hold her head up and face whatever may come. The best she could do was muffle the sound of her crying in her cape that she clutched to her face.

John pulled her as close as he could. His comforting touch dried up her tears, lending her his strength. She already dreaded the moment she would have to return that strength to him.

SIXTEEN

As Carlyle and Jimmy the Bruise conferred in the doorway, John massaged his temple, a vain attempt to assuage what he really ought to call a migraine. He kept one arm about her, but that would have to come to an end all too soon. She knew him, it seemed, better than he knew himself. Over the course of the past few days, she had proved to be an astute judge of character, and he would miss her insights when he left the Amish community and returned to his own home.

His home. Where was it, exactly? If they got out of this alive, he would have to go home, wherever it was. He might recall enough to testify, but he still couldn't remember where he lived. Could he go to his parents? He knew the names of his parents, but he would not know them if he ran into them on the street. Surely, hopefully, it would all return by the time he needed that information.

He hadn't taken his eyes off their two captors since he had pushed the buggy into the barn. They had promised to bolt John and Sarah in and burn the barn down, but so far, they just seemed to be arguing. All hope was gone for rescue. In good weather, an *Englisch* automobile at the schoolhouse would have raised suspicion. But no one was out in this snowstorm. There was no one to notice.

A sharp pain pierced his skull, and John resumed rubbing his temple with his free hand.

"Is your head hurting again?" Sarah seemed to have calmed after her cry, and now her soothing voice forced his attention.

"Yeah. It's worse this time."

Sarah nodded toward Carlyle and The Bruise. "Why do they wait?"

"I don't know." Angry heat rose within his chest, and the idea of rushing them flitted through the haze of his headache. "But we're stuck. We certainly can't look for a way out when they're still here."

If they survived, could he ever leave the world behind and be Amish? Or was too much of the world in him already? Could the Lord help him with his attitude and word choice? Of course He could. But would He if he asked? Sure, Sarah worried and got anxious, but through all their trouble and turmoil the past few days, she had seemed…unflappable. Composed and collected. At peace.

His chest ached with the desire to have that kind of calm peacefulness. God could do anything, couldn't He? Especially with a soul that was completely surrendered to Him.

The migraine radiated from his temples across the top of his head, and without knowing what else to do to ease the pain, he closed his eyes and continued to rub his forehead. It wasn't helping, but it wasn't hurting, either, and it gave him something to do with his free hand. There certainly wasn't any need for surveillance. They were in the clutches of the enemy.

"Are you remembering more? Is that bringing the ache?"

"I'm certainly trying, but so much remains fuzzy. I have a little bit that's clear, but then it blurs around the edges and disappears completely."

"Maybe if you talk about what you remember, that could help, both your memories and your headache. And that is information you will need if—when—we get through this."

He shrugged, wishing that roll of his shoulders could toss off his worries. But a glance at their captors in the doorway only tightened his muscles. "I suppose it won't hurt."

He paused, trying to gather up the fraying edges. But it was useless. Everything was disjointed. There was no good place to start, to try to put it all together. "I remember a feeling of bitterness from when I was very young. I think my parents must have left their Amish faith with great resentment toward God. It's only bits and pieces, more so images, that have come back after what Mary told us. A little sister, a baby girl wrapped in a blanket, but there were problems. Mom cried. A lot. My grandfather—I guess that would be Mary's husband—had a long gray beard. It strikes me that he was very conservative, and my mom and dad seemed to be upset with him, although they did not talk much."

Sarah nodded her encouragement. "*Jah*, *Mammi* Mary said that her husband—your grandfather—would not let them go for medical help. Finally, your *daed* decided to go anyway, but it was too late."

John worried a fold of her cape between his thumb and first finger. "I remember a tiny casket. And there was so much crying. And anger. I remember lots of anger. At each other. At God."

Quiet engulfed them for a moment. John continued to stare at Carlyle and The Bruise. One was on the phone now. It was only a matter of time before they enacted their plan, and John's mind raced to figure out a way to escape.

"That was a long time ago. It will not help to hold on to resentment."

She was right, of course. But he could only stare through the open barn door at the snow swirling, trying to formulate an escape plan, as the sun set quickly behind the clouds. Were they waiting for the cover of darkness?

A new memory pinged, and he startled. "You know what? My dad told me his parents were dead. I remember now. That's what I grew up believing."

"I am sorry, John."

"Throughout my childhood, my parents rejected any kind of faith. I never went to church. And when I did have friends who tried to witness to me, I became too afraid to tell my parents because they ridiculed my friends who believed." He paused, letting his mind run to the edge of that memory, trying to absorb as much as he could before it disappeared into the amnesia. An image surfaced of him on his knees by his bed in a dorm room. "I became a believer in college, through a campus ministry. But because of my parents' bitterness, I've kept my faith a secret from them."

If Sarah was shocked by any of his memories, she didn't show it. There was that peaceful calm again, an aura that surrounded her and drew him in. "Pray for them, and let *Gott* work His will."

"Jah." This beautiful Amish woman had been a positive influence on him.

Carlyle and The Bruise moved to their vehicle but left the barn door open with a clear view of John and Sarah. This walk down memory lane was, most likely, not going to end with a happily-ever-after.

"They are still there?" She didn't have to specify who she was talking about.

"Of course. Their lives are at stake, and so that means ours are, as well." Another flash, like lightning, invaded his thoughts. Images of equipment, the odor of ink, the clanging of machinery. "Remember I said that Jimmy the Bruise is a counterfeiter? I need to testify at the trial because I was undercover. I infiltrated his crime ring. The case could falter if I can't testify. That's why he's so eager to eliminate me." An urgency like he had never felt before rose up within his chest. "What makes it all worse for him is that I can identify the other men involved and testify to their criminal activities as well as provide positive information on contacts for money laundering, not to mention equipment and materials used, as well as their locations." He ran through a mental list of names and information, details that Sarah didn't need to be bothered with.

"What about the man called Carlyle? He is a police officer?"

"Yeah, on the take. That means he's accepting cash payments from the criminals in exchange for keeping the police away from the investigation. If the ring goes down, they'll rat him out and he'll go down, as well." He had to get them free, and the sooner the better.

"How did you discover him?" Sarah glanced through the door, an odd mix of curiosity and repugnance on her pretty face.

And the more he remembered, the greater the chasm between her Amish world and his *Englisch* one grew.

"A hunch. My captain suspected something odd, since we never seemed to get anywhere with an investigation. So, we kept it quiet, and I went in alone. It didn't take long to learn the identity of the dirty cop and just how deep his involvement was. The problem was, I had to withdraw too soon. I never got to report Carlyle to my captain. In the department, he still appears innocent with a clean record. I thought more cops were involved than just

Carlyle, but I ran out of time. It had seemed at the time that the tentacles of the counterfeiting ring snaked further through the police department than just Carlyle, but I wasn't able to discover exactly who was involved. That means I'm not sure now who to trust, except for one officer. One friend. He's the one I'll call."

"But how did you end up out here in our Amish community?"

"I was stressed. Needed some time off before the trial." He pulled off his hat and ran his hand through his hair. "I think I thought that getting out of town would be a good idea. Apparently, I was right that I was in danger. But the danger followed me anyway."

John leaned forward, squinting toward the gathering dark outside. Carlyle and Jimmy the Bruise were returning from their vehicle, lighters in hand. The moment was at hand.

Snow flung into the barn and stuck to their captors. Sarah leaned against John and swiped a hand over her forehead. This was it.

She had had some good times in this widespread community, cultivated some lifelong relationships, made mountains of memories. But her time here was almost over. And if she did survive, she and Lyddie would move back to Lancaster County. Even now, her letter back to her mother rested in her apron pocket, jabbing her in the leg when she shifted her position, a persistent reminder that *Gott*'s will was best.

Her time with John was also almost over. She most likely wouldn't make it through the night, let alone make it back to Lancaster County. Her life was at an end. There was no way out, and it seemed for sure and for certain that the men quickly approaching them would achieve their goal.

Had *Gott* decided it was her time to go? Apparently so. Grief coursed through her. But a second emotion also ran through her veins. Gratitude.

She was grateful that *Gott*, in His wisdom and grace, had seen fit to give her two loves in one short lifetime.

Two loves?

Jah, she had loved her husband dearly and did not regret a minute spent with him.

But *Gott* had given her another love. Whether or not it could work was up to John. He probably was not willing to leave his *Englisch* life. So be it. But if neither survived what was coming, she at least wanted him to know how she felt. He had taken the huge risk back at the schoolhouse to reveal his heart's feelings to her. She should return the sentiment while she still had the breath to speak the words.

She would toss out her earlier logic that she saw no point in voicing emotions. She must have been *ferhoodled* by fright. The heart sometimes did not know logic.

Sarah loved him. John's desire to rejoin the Amish church was uncertain, even unlikely. But his care for her had helped her see that a loving *Gott* would not want her to be miserable. For that, she was grateful.

What she ought to do was clear. Tell him that she loved him. But her throat constricted as the men quickly approached.

John released her and took her hand in his as, together, they faced Carlyle and Jimmy the Bruise. She was grateful for the warmth of human touch in what would most likely be her final moments.

SEVENTEEN

The snow beat furiously against the barn door as it swung on its hinges. How many days had it been since John had first arrived here in the Amish community? His mind couldn't quite figure it out, but it hadn't been that long ago. Lyddie had told about pulling him on the sled as he lay unconscious.

Now he was stuck, against his own volition. His arrival here had been the result of a lifesaving mission. His departure was to be the result of a life-ending mission.

Low muttering swirled about as Carlyle and Jimmy the Bruise pulled their collars up against the weather. "That storm will be helpful."

"Yeah, it'll cover our tracks, but the fire will still burn strong."

John couldn't tell which one said what, but did it matter? Neither could wait to light the match.

The barn added some relief against the storm as he followed Sarah deeper inside to join Thunder and Lightning in their stalls. He met Sarah's gaze as she stood near Thunder's muzzle, intending to say something encouraging to strengthen her. But instead, her eyes burned bright with determination.

"I will not remove their bridles." Her whisper was barely audible. "If we can find a way of escape, we will take the horses, as well."

John ran his hand down the length of Thunder as he exited the stall. The sooner he could identify potential exits, the better their chances of escape once these goons were gone.

"I'll check the perimeter," The Bruise was saying near the door. "Make sure there's no way out and all exits are blocked or locked."

Carlyle nodded. "I'll keep an eye on 'em here."

Jimmy jogged out into the snow, and Carlyle turned to see John. "So, you know our plan. It's a pretty good one, don't you think? I'm sure the Fort Wayne Police Department will give you a proper and honorable police funeral. I'll be your pallbearer. Maybe it'll be a memorial service, depending on how much of you is left. Either way, you'll be gone but not forgotten." A wicked grin slithered across his face.

Sarah had apparently finished whatever she was doing with the horses, and now she stood next to him. Her free hand slid into his, and he grasped her warmth. Whatever happened next, they were in this together, the two of them.

Carlyle stared for a moment at their intertwined hands. "Oh, now, Jed. Don't tell me you've gone and fallen for this pretty little Amish girl. Too bad that relationship won't go anywhere."

The Bruise reappeared in the doorway. "All's secure. And that troublemaking dog seems to be long gone after I chased him off."

With weapon in hand, the officer waved them back. "Back you go. Like I said, you won't be tied. But not to worry, there's no way out. One thing about the Amish, they know how to build a sturdy barn. But it's still wood. It'll burn fast enough."

The officer's gun trained on John and Sarah, Carlyle and Jimmy the Bruise stepped backward toward the door. Without another word, they both stepped outside. The door slammed shut. John raced forward in time to hear a scraping, as if they were securing it with a two-by-four or a strong limb. Either one would burn up in the fire, leaving no evidence of foul play.

John wasn't sure what they would do on the outside to get the fire going, but there were many ways to start a fire, even in a snowstorm. The danger was the same. Even as he stood there with those few thoughts, staring at the door, smoke began to filter in around the bottom edge. A moment later, a flicker of fire began to lick at the base of the door.

Adrenaline spiked in his arteries. His heart pumping and thumping, he rushed back to Sarah. "Whatever they're doing out there, it's fast. We have fire."

A mist formed around Sarah's eyes. "We're locked in. There's no way out. A barn can be completely engulfed, and horses can die from smoke inhalation within less than ten minutes."

"Then I'll hurry." He squeezed her upper arm. "Stay here. Now that Carlyle and Jimmy are gone, I'm going to search the perimeter for a way out." It may be a familiar barn to her, but that didn't mean that she knew every loose board, every knothole, every animal in-and-out.

He dashed around the inside edge of the structure, pushing on walls, trying doorknobs, searching for tools. As he worked his way through a tool room, he grabbed an ax.

Less than two minutes later, he returned to find Sarah swiping at her eyes with her apron, looking as if she fought desperately to stay strong and not let her mist turn into a waterfall of tears.

John hitched up his grip on the ax and then ran his free hand down the length of Sarah's arm, catching her hand. "Dry your tears. We're not going to die in this fire, and neither are Thunder and Lightning. I've found a way out."

Hope fluttered in Sarah's stomach as she looked up into John's shining green eyes. Could it really be? *Please, Gott!* Her death had been nigh, but now here stood a handsome and capable man telling her she was saved.

John dropped her hand to grip the ax, and a sudden chill shook her, despite the heat from the growing flames. She forced positive thoughts into her mind. Everything would be all right. She had to believe that.

"It never hurts to have an ax with you, for fighting fires or fighting the bad guys." Nervousness dimpled around his eyes, but he seemed to force a smile to reassure her. "The walls and doors are solid wood, so I can't chop through those in the few minutes we have before the smoke gets to be too much. But, Carlyle and his partner in crime forgot about the hayloft at the back of the barn."

"*Jah*, of course, the little door used to toss out the hay. It is to our advantage, then, that those men are not farmers." She followed John toward the ladder. Flames were inching farther up the door and the walls, and a small bunch of straw had caught. It would not be long before the entire barn was engulfed. Her breath caught in her throat at the acrid aroma of smoke.

John clambered up a few rungs, looking back to make sure she was coming behind. Smoke was beginning to billow upward. Sarah, despite shaking legs, stepped up to the first rung. Halfway up, he called down with a wobbly voice, "I'm not sure how we'll get to the ground, but at least we won't burn up."

"Oh!" A drum seemed to be beating in her chest. "The rope!" They could shimmy down the rope to the ground below. In the summertime, with the doors below open wide, children could swing on the rope in and out of the first level of the barn. Lyddie had begged time and time again to swing, but Sarah just never had the stomach for it. It seemed too dangerous. So many possible injuries just waiting to happen.

But now was not the time for caution. Even a broken leg after plummeting to the ground would be better than dying in the fire. A broken limb would heal. And surely the rope would provide some assistance in getting down to the ground.

With hay stacked neatly all around, John led them across the loft and to the door. It was secured with a chain and padlock, but a couple of blows from the ax broke through the wooden door handle. He slipped the chain off and swung the small door open, and a chill blew in for a moment. But then the fire, fed by the oxygen, roared up the ladder. Sarah inched toward the door, desperate for a gulp of the fresh air. Already she felt like she had smoke and soot all over her.

John scanned the yard and the nearby woods and, seeing no one, dropped the ax down to the ground. "So no one gets hurt on the way down." He tugged on the rope and then hung on it, testing it for strength. Seemingly satisfied, he tossed the end out the door. It barely touched the ground. "I'll go first, to make sure it'll hold."

A moment later, John was on the ground. He held his arms up as if to catch Sarah, a signal that it was her turn and the rope would hold.

With one final look around the loft, Sarah grasped the rope, a fold of her skirt in each hand to protect against rope burns. With a gasp stuck in her throat, she stepped out of the loft and into the air. The gasp let loose as her hands slipped on the twine, her strength not adequate for the task. With barely both hands on the rope, she slid down to the bottom at a blurring speed. A moment later, strong arms held her. John had caught her in his embrace.

With her feet firmly on the ground again, snow swirling all around but doing nothing to stop the fire, Sarah glanced around the yard. Surely, Carlyle and Jimmy the Bruise had left.

"The horses." Sarah nodded as John breathed deeply of the fresh air and then stepped toward the back barn doors, leaving a void in his absence. Several strong ax blows to the solid crossbeams securing the barn door swung it open. The influx of fresh air fueled the fire, and flames leaped out the doors at the ceiling and around the doorway.

Pulling away from her surveillance, Sarah quickly untied her apron and jerked it off. "Here," she called to John before he could enter the barn. She folded it and knelt to wet the apron with some snow. "You must cover the horses' eyes, or they will not follow."

John rushed inside, leaping away from the flames that seemed to chase him. Too many heartbeats later, he reappeared, leading Lightning. The door swung shut just as he pulled away the blindfold and pushed the horse through. Sarah jumped forward to catch the door before it could hit the horse in the muzzle, and Lightning trotted free of the barn, circling around in the yard.

With one animal safe, John reentered the blazing barn. Sarah stood at the door, ready to hold it open, her eyes watering from the smoke and her throat aching for a long drink of fresh water. Just as the flames leaped larger inside, John appeared with Thunder. He pulled on the lead rope, digging his heels into the floor to lead the frightened animal out.

Heat closed in on Sarah as the horse finally rushed past her and out into the yard.

"Sarah!" John pointed at her skirt.

The hem of her dress was on fire. A ringing in her ears clanged loudly, and she saw John's lips moving, but she could not hear his voice. Flames licked up her skirt, but she stood immobile. Before she could form a coherent response, she was down on the ground.

John shoved the damp, soiled apron at her and kneeled at her feet. As he scooped large handfuls of snow on her hem, she tamped at it with the piece of cloth.

The fire of her skirt was soon extinguished, and John pulled her to her feet. "Let's get the horses and get out of here."

She could only nod as she rubbed her hands together.

Lightning continued to prance around the yard back of the barn. But Thunder, with ears pinned back, tossed his head up and down. He stamped his feet in the snow, panic radiating from him. John spoke softly to him, but as Sarah crossed the yard in the deep snow to calm him, the horse stepped toward her. She held up both hands, her cry of "John!" trusting and desperate.

With a loud whinny, Thunder reared up, his hooves flailing over her head. Sarah froze. Even over the roar of the fire, she could hear her own scream.

EIGHTEEN

Sarah's scream pulsed through her head, only extinguished when John pulled her to safety. Both fell in the snow as the horse trotted away from the barn.

With trembling hands, Sarah accepted John's help up, and they huddled together. "We must let the horses calm. They are panicked from the fire."

She nodded as she stroked her own arms, whispering a prayer and praying her own words would soothe her, as well. John's strong arms encompassed her, but Sarah also kept an eye on Thunder and Lightning. They were a crucial form of transportation and could not be lost, especially since they provided a speed that could not be achieved on foot. The barn was destroyed, or would be, by the time the fire was extinguished. But as she counted her blessings, she numbered quite a few. They had escaped, unharmed. John had saved both the horses. Lyddie was still safe. Between the intensity of the fire and the snowstorm, the bad guys should have been long gone. But the tension would not flow out of her. Her muscles bunched, and her hands shook as she thought of the long trek through the woods to get to the phone shanty.

The canter of the horses slowed, and Sarah broke free to approach the animals at a gentle pace. Grasping a lead rope in each hand, she led them farther away from the fire and behind some overgrown mulberry bushes where they would not be visible from the front of the schoolhouse or the road.

"I'm sorry there's no time to rest, but we need to move." John joined her behind the bush, his voice urgent. "We still need to get to the phone as quickly as possible. And I don't trust staying here, just in case they come back or are watching from afar."

"We will have to ride Thunder and Lightning then. The Amish do not often ride their horses. They are for pulling. So even without the fire, we would not have had saddles. Can you ride bareback?"

"I'll have to learn." His gaze swept down her long skirt. "What about you?"

"I learned when I was younger. My mother was not happy with me for riding, but I loved it. The freedom of it. The speed. The wind. It is true that it is not easy for an Amish woman to ride a horse, but my skirt is full enough for some give, and since it is winter, I have thick leggings on underneath." She looked from the ground to the height of the horse. "I could use a hand up, though, please."

He laced his fingers together as she hiked her skirt up and bunched it in one hand. It felt odd and uncomfortable, but what was that cliché? Desperate times called for desperate measures, and she certainly was desperate to get John to that telephone. With the other hand on his sturdy shoulder, she pulled herself up onto the horse. After she settled her full skirt about her, she looked around, but there was no sign of Carlyle and The Bruise. She tucked around herself a barn blanket John had managed to save from the fire.

John on Thunder, after receiving directions from Sarah, led them into the woods. Exhausted by the events of the day and warmed by the blanket, Sarah was desperate for sleep. Weariness enveloped her, but anxiety kept her eyes open.

The neighbor with the telephone was not far by *Englisch* standards, but the storm would slow the horses down. And though the wind had lessened within the trees, the snow lay deep. At least John knew who he could trust now. With the neighbor out of town visiting family in Ohio, John and Sarah would be alone at the neighbor's barn and not bring trouble on yet another family in the community. Besides, he would not mind if they sought shelter in his barn. The telephone was available for anyone to use as long as they paid their part of the bill.

The Amish took care of each other. That was what people did who loved each other.

Like John? Did she dare to hope that perhaps John loved her? For sure and for certain, he had done everything within his abilities to take care of her and assure her safety.

No. He was a police officer, most likely a good one. The doctor had said that despite the amnesia, John's instincts honed through training and his muscle memory would have remained intact. So, he was doing his job. Protecting people who needed him. That was all. He had said he cared, but wasn't that in his job description?

John turned and offered her a hopeful smile, and her heart flittered in her chest like the snowflakes in the storm. "The snow will muffle the sound of the horses. And although we'll leave tracks, I think they'll be covered up quickly because the snow is falling so thickly."

He pointed to the path behind Thunder, and she turned to see what sort of trail she was leaving on Lightning. But just as she verified that the snow was, indeed, filling in their steps, a tree just a couple of feet from her exploded. Bark flew in every direction. A piece smacked her in the cheek. Sarah spun back forward and hunched over, making herself as small as possible.

"They spotted us!" John's whisper seemed to echo through the woods. "They're shooting at us!"

A warm, sticky substance trickled down her cheek. Sarah leaned down to a corner of the blanket and pressed it to the spot. It came away with a circle of blood on it. The tree bark must have broken the skin, but it didn't seem serious.

John leaned forward on his mount. "Come on! Farther into the woods."

Those thugs must have seen them slip into the trees. And even though the men had to be on foot, John and Sarah couldn't outrun a bullet, not riding bareback and not with the fury of an increasing snowstorm beating at them.

Sarah huddled down farther, both for protection and for warmth. She urged Lightning ahead, and the horse picked up the pace. But with the snow flying even thicker and the temperature continuing to drop, time worked against them. They could last in the elements only so long, but they had no choice but to continue, no matter how long it took to reach shelter and safety.

Another bullet blasted into a nearby bush, the last few leaves from autumn flying off. Thunder sidestepped, and John stroked his neck as snow landed on his own head and eyelashes. His vision blurred as the snow melted on his face, and he swiped his hand across his eyes to clear away the wetness.

John peered behind him. Sarah was close behind on Lightning, leaning into the wind, her eyes squinting into the snowstorm. There was no sign of the shooter, although with the encroaching darkness and the thickness of the snowfall, he hadn't expected to see anyone.

At least there was no way those men could drive their car through the woods in the snow. And unless they had snowmobiles tucked away in the trunk, they would be on foot. They surely couldn't follow very far, not in that cold and the snow. He and Sarah would have the advantage with Thunder and Lightning to carry them and the horses' body heat to help keep them warm.

John held his mount back and turned to Sarah. "You go ahead. Lead the way and stay down as best you can."

Sarah inched ahead, but John rode close behind, pushing them deeper into the woods. Bare limbs scratched at them, and Sarah did her best to push them out of the way and hold them back, but a few snapped in his face. At the feel of warm stickiness, he feared he had a wound that matched Sarah's.

A crash came from behind them, followed by muffled voices. Carlyle and The Bruise hadn't given up yet, then. That meant that now John and Sarah were battling cold and snow as well as the two men who wanted them dead.

God, help! Did it take more than that? He suspected not, given their dire circumstances. But as he leaned over his horse and scanned the surrounding woods, he prayed for protection. Sarah would tell him that *Gott* would protect them if it was His will to do so, and she would be right. If they could just get to that telephone, he could summon law enforcement who would serve and protect.

But would they make it to the phone shanty alive?

A sliver of the setting sun filtered through the cloud cover, creating shifting shadows. John pointed to the closest shadow, and Sarah headed in that direction. The extra darkness might hide them temporarily, but what they really needed was shelter. Their speed had slowed, also, because they were riding bareback. John must have had some experience with horseback riding because he seemed to know what to do although he had no memory of it. Still, though, bareback was slippery enough without adding the moisture of snow. Some moments, it was all John could do to stay on. The thickness of the falling snow cut their visibility and further slowed them.

John drew close and pointed to a stand of evergreen trees. "Over there."

Sarah nodded and turned Lightning in that direction as the high-intensity beam of a flashlight swept across the snow just a few feet behind them.

"Go! Faster!" He kept his voice to a hoarse whisper.

John's heart thumped a wild beat inside his chest as the stream of light from the flashlight chased them to the cluster of trees. Craning his neck to watch behind, he thought a beam of light glanced briefly on his horse's foot. But the trees were straight ahead, and a moment later, Sarah and Lightning slipped behind the stand. He quickly followed on Thunder. Finally, he allowed himself to exhale a breath he felt like he had been holding since they left the barn.

He didn't have to motion to Sarah to stay quiet. She hugged the blanket around herself and stared at him with eyes wide with fright. Through the branches, he could just make out the two men on foot. They swept their beams of light in a wide arc and stepped forward about twenty feet apart, communicating with hand motions. One beam swept across the evergreens, and he jerked back, holding his breath to keep from making a single sound. Thankfully, Thunder cooperated and remained still and silent, as well.

Eventually, after what seemed so long he half expected the sun to rise, the men began to move to the side and back in the general direction from which they had come.

Sarah's whisper sounded behind him, loud in the hush of the snow. "Are they gone?"

After one last visual sweep of the area in front of the trees, he turned Thunder to face her. "I think they've probably turned around. Despite the cold, we ought to stay here a bit longer, just to make sure that they are gone and we don't lead them to the neighbor's barn."

"*Jah*, I agree."

"Are you warm enough to wait it out awhile?" In the faint moonlight that snuck through the clouds, the pink of her cheeks accentuated her beauty.

"I am getting warmth from Lightning. I am fine."

Thunder stomped in the snow, perhaps because he was tired of standing still, perhaps to get the blood flowing again. Snow continued to swirl around them and add to the heaps of snow already on the tree branches and stuck against the tree trunks. John swept the snow from his shoulders and shook it out of his hair, water droplets clinging to his hands.

Thunder pawed at the ground and then turned in a circle. John clung to his mane so he wouldn't slip off.

"He is restless," Sarah whispered, her breath puffing a cloud. "He is tired of standing still and is ready to go."

"I'm ready to go, too, to get to that phone. But we're hidden here. I hesitate to take off and then be spotted. But Thunder is making it hard to stay upright." The horse swayed again, toward Sarah, causing John to grasp at Lightning's reins and neck.

Lightning also shifted, and the two horses bumped. John leaned to pat Lightning's neck and steady her. Sarah held out her hand, and John grabbed it for support. The softness of her hand startled him after the harshness of the chase, and her skin was surprisingly warm in the cold winter night. He shivered, but it wasn't from the cold.

As a few flurries continued to flutter down, the clouds parted. Moonlight flooded the clearing behind the trees, and he stared at her. Her skin was pinked from the cold, and her lips were parted slightly, her breath puffing out in small clouds.

With only the smallest flurry of thought, like the snowflakes that continued to drift about them, he leaned in closer, his lips almost touching hers. Without hesitation, she closed the space. Their lips met, and hers were as soft and warm as he had anticipated. The cold around him disappeared, and warmth flooded him.

I love her.

What? The startling realization forced him away from her. He pushed his foot against the horse and moved away, the winter chill seeping into the space between them. Before he turned, she touched her fingers to her lips, her expression a mixture of pleasure and confusion.

He urged Thunder a few steps away, his

back to Sarah. He peered through the trees to make sure Carlyle and Jimmy had not returned, but he really needed the distance from her.

He loved her? It was true. Through the past few days, he had witnessed her compassion for others, her devotion to her daughter, her work ethic, her sweetness. What more could a man want?

But what could come of it? Since he had been able to infiltrate the counterfeiting ring and gather that information, he must, at the very least, be somewhat good at his job. But even with the return of his memory, there was still so much uncertainty in his skills after the period of not knowing himself. It felt wonderful to remember everything, but his confidence was unstable, both in himself and in his faith. If he had not even known himself, how could he know God and His will for his life? Maybe, with time, he could have more confidence in his abilities. He might have a job to go back to, but he'd feel like a rookie all over again.

He could not ask Sarah to leave her Amish faith to become a police officer's wife. Never. And if he left his job in law enforcement and joined the Amish community, how could he support a family?

Lord, You've brought me this far. If I'm to believe in Your sovereignty, then that means You've led me to Sarah. But what now? What do I do?

As he prayed, a fresh infusion of encouragement flittered down on him. A warm blanket of peace and joy filled him that could only have been from the Lord. With a *tch-tch* to the horse, he spun back to Sarah. She had her face to the sky, letting the last of the flurries alight on her face.

"I should have said it earlier," he whispered.

She fluttered open her eyes and looked at him. He shot up a prayer that that was hope he saw in her eyes, a hope that was probably mirrored in his own.

"I love you."

He leaned in close again and claimed her lips, the touch warming him in the bitter cold. Where this relationship might lead, he had no idea. But for the moment, being in the moonlight with her and her acceptance of his kiss were enough.

NINETEEN

For sure and for certain, that kiss would warm her up.

But it couldn't last forever. When John pulled away, his mount shifting feet again and swaying him apart from Sarah, the cold invaded, even more bitter than before. The absence of his lips against hers chilled her to the bone.

The little warmth she received from the horse wasn't enough any longer to combat the snow and the wind. The shivering began in her arms but soon consumed her entire body.

John quickly pulled his blanket off and wrapped it around her.

"*Ach*, no, John. You will freeze." She began to remove the blanket, but he held out his hand in protest.

"I insist. We've been out here for quite a while with no sign of Carlyle or The Bruise, so let's hurry to that neighbor's barn. I'll warm up there."

She urged Lightning forward, John on Thunder following close behind. Only the moonlight and the peaceful silence accompanied them. Perhaps the threat really was gone, and their safety would be secured once they reached the telephone in the barn.

Shivers still consumed her now and then, but they soon rode out of the trees. The barn stood silhouetted against the night sky. Safety at last.

John dismounted and opened the barn doors. Warmth enveloped her as she entered, the wind and the snow and the chill left outside. John led Thunder to the nearest stall and quickly closed the doors.

As he helped Sarah dismount, she cherished the strength and sturdiness inherent in his hands as they encircled her waist. He had been a good protector and would be into the future…except, the telephone was in a shanty just adjacent to the barn and it would all be over soon.

Keeping the blanket wrapped around herself, Sarah showed John the door to the telephone. "It is just there. You can make your call and summon help."

"Right. Be right back." He ran his hand down her upper arm, then turned toward the door.

John returned a few minutes later and joined her near the horses.

"Did you reach who you wanted?" She kept her voice low, a practice she had adopted over the last few days of intense caution.

"Yes. Help is on the way." He scrubbed a hand over his chin. "What about weapons? For protection. Does the neighbor have a hunting rifle?"

"*Jah*. Most every Amish man has that." She moved to a nearby cabinet, her heart heavy. Inside sat a rifle with extra boxes of ammunition. All this time spent together, and John's first instinct was still to find a gun. He wasn't changed at all. Any hope she had had of a future with him in the Amish church was now shattered. "Please leave it there. It is for hunting only. I know you come from a profession that includes the use of weapons and violence. But *Gott* will protect us."

She clutched the bodice of her dress. Her heart felt like it would be torn into little pieces. John was so different, coming from the *Englisch* world. How could he ever choose to be a part of the *we* of the Amish community, let alone the *we* of—did she dare even to think it?—Jed and Sarah Miller? The *we* of a family with her and Lyddie?

No. She would not torture herself. She pushed it from her mind, although it took all her mental energy.

But the request was made. Now he stood staring at her. Love shone in his eyes, but it seemed there was also a sadness. Was he realizing just how different they were, how unequally yoked, and how impossible a permanent relationship would be?

He hesitated, seemingly torn between what was probably instinct and what, she prayed, was his faith working in him.

John knew what he needed to do, and Sarah was the encouragement to do it.

Amish vows would have to wait until the appropriate time, but he could, and he would, reassure her now. He would respect her and her faith, a faith that he wanted to be his again.

He stepped away from the cabinet where the rifle rested and closer to her, drawing her into his arms. "Sarah, I've already said I care about you. But I also want to say—"

The crash of the barn door interrupted him and sent a pounding to his chest like he couldn't remember ever having experienced. Now, not only was his own life on the line, but also the life of the woman he loved.

He had taken too long. Too long to hide in the woods. Too long to finish their journey and reach the barn. Too long to make his telephone call.

And now the rifle still sat in the cabinet, too far away to reach.

The chilled wind and flurries of snow blew in with the two men, weapons pointed at John and Sarah. A sneer bedecked the angry face of Simon Carlyle, the dirty cop who had come to finish the job and eliminate the man who could testify against him. The black-and-blue birthmark of Jimmy the Bruise wrapped around his neck and down his arm, seeming to pulsate with Jimmy's rage.

As Jimmy pointed his weapon at Sarah, John grabbed her hand. Whatever happened, he wouldn't let her face it alone. A wicked smile snaked across Jimmy's fleshy lips. "So, she's your girl now? Love has blossomed under the pressure of the chase? Okay, then. You can watch her die first."

Carlyle tossed a glance at The Bruise. "Jimmy, you yap entirely too much. Get it done already. I'm sick of this problem."

"Fine. First, I'll have Jed here dig the hole

for his girl. Then he can dig his own hole. All I have to do is fill the dirt in." His malicious smile grew.

John let Sarah's hand loose and raised both in surrender. "Now, guys, can't we work something out?" As far as he could tell, neither Carlyle nor Jimmy knew he had called the police. If he could just keep them talking, perhaps he could keep Sarah alive until reinforcements arrived.

"What do you mean, Jed? You're in? Ready to live a little beyond that miserable policeman's salary?"

John forced a casual shrug. "What did you have in mind?"

Jimmy growled at Carlyle, but Carlyle continued. "Well…"

A sudden movement flashed behind the two men, at the door. Something beige and brown and white. Something large. Law enforcement couldn't be there yet. John darted his gaze to see what it was. It was Snowball, teeth bared and eyes narrowed, ready for a fight.

Just as recognition flickered in Jimmy's eyes that John had seen something behind him, Jimmy turned. The dog attacked with a leap, flying right at his face.

Snowball's growl forced Carlyle to turn

to see what was causing the commotion. As his attention refocused, John lunged for him. With a hand on Carlyle's wrist, John twisted the man's arm, but the weapon fired. A bullet shot up to the ceiling. Sarah screamed and covered her ears as she dropped to the ground. With one strong wrench, John took control of Carlyle's gun.

His hands covering his face, Jimmy tried to protect himself from the large and vicious dog. As The Bruise cowered on the floor, his knees pulled to his chest, John retrieved his weapon, now holding both guns on their two attackers.

"Sarah, the dog!"

Sarah sniffled and sat up. "Snowball! No!" She grabbed the dog's collar and pulled, stroking her back gently and speaking more softly to calm her.

Jimmy whimpered as he pulled his bloody hands away from his face.

"Rope, Sarah?"

She motioned to Snowball to stay. The dog seemed to have calmed, now that the two men weren't threatening her any longer. Sarah stepped away to riffle through a couple of cabinets, returning with a length of cord that was more than enough to tie up Carlyle and Jimmy the Bruise.

The faint scream of sirens sounded outside. A few moments later, the barn filled with several police officers, and Carlyle and Jimmy the Bruise were taken into custody. John handed over their weapons to the nearest uniformed officer and then sagged against the rail of the stall, his legs wilting underneath him.

With the quilt still draped over her shoulders, Sarah approached him. "May we step outside now? For some fresh air and a change of scenery?"

"Jah." A smile wobbled across his lips as he spoke the Pennsylvania German. "Sounds *gut.*"

Confusion flittered across her beautiful face, followed by a shy smile.

With fresh blankets thrown over their shoulders, John led her to the outdoor porch of the neighbor's house. Snowball followed and sat next to Sarah, reaching up to try to lick her hand. "The police will have some questions for you eventually. But you're safe now. It's all over. Life can go back to normal."

"Normal?" Sarah stared at the ground. "We are leaving Indiana. Normal for Lyddie and for me will be back in Pennsylvania." Something sparkled on her cheek. Was it a tear?

"No." His pulse raced within him as he

pulled Sarah into his embrace. "Let me finish what I was beginning to say before we were interrupted." Snowball barked, and John ran a hand over her head. He grabbed that moment to swallow over a sudden lump in his throat and toss up a quick prayer. "Sarah, I've said I care about you. I care about Lyddie, too. I also said that I love you. I love you both. Now that my memory has returned, I believe the Lord is leading me back to my Amish heritage. I want to speak to the bishop about joining the church."

A gasp escaped Sarah, and her arms found their way around his neck to pull him into a tight hug. "That is *wunderbar!*" She released him and pulled away, her beautiful face pink, probably with embarrassment.

Snow began to flit down again, but this time it was a gentle free fall of large flakes.

"I don't know yet what I'll do to earn my keep, but I'm grateful for how you've helped me find my way back, with a little encouragement. And—" he cleared his throat, fighting the lump that continued to grow "—I know where I'd like to settle."

This was it. This was the moment. What if she said *no*? What if he had misread her, and she was only helping him because it was her responsibility as an Amish woman who was true to her faith?

But as he looked down at her, it seemed that hopefulness shone from her soft brown eyes. As the snow flurried down around them, the chill of the winter air making him pull her even closer, he thought he could smell the aroma of cinnamon and home and hearth in her brown curls. God's peace settled on him like a warm quilt.

"I've already said it, but I'll say it again and again. I love you, Sarah. I need to wrap up a number of things, including testifying at the trial in a couple of weeks. And I need to figure out how I'm going to earn a living once I'm no longer a police officer. But if you agree, I'd like to write to you in the interim."

Silence seemed to settle around them, broken only by the pounding of his heart as he waited. Then, like the sun breaking free from the winter storm clouds, a smile lit her face. "*Jah*, I would like that. And John? I love you, too."

EPILOGUE

Two weeks later

Sarah plunged her hands back into the hot, soapy water and grasped another plate. A snowmobile hummed in the distance as she scrubbed, rinsed and placed the plate on the towel to dry. A letter sat propped up on the windowsill, but this one wasn't from her mother urging her to come back to Pennsylvania to marry again.

This letter was from her love, declaring that he was counting the days until he could return to the Amish community and to her. In fact, two other letters rested behind the first. The name John had served him well during his amnesia, but now he was Jed again, a good, strong name for a fine man.

She glanced at the calendar again, but it was still the same date as it had been five minutes ago when she had looked at it…

the day of the trial of Simon Carlyle and the counterfeiter called Jimmy the Bruise. Today was the day for Jed's crucial testimony that would, he hoped, help return a guilty verdict for the men.

Snowball barked from outside, and the door opened with a gust of cold winter wind, blowing in Lyddie in her black winter cape and bonnet. "*Mamm*, may I go to the sledding hill? I will take Snowball with me."

Sarah smiled at the plea of her daughter. Her daughter knew exactly how to ask for something by including her protective dog, for sure and for certain.

"*Jah*, but be back before sunset. That is not long from now."

"*Danki, Mamm.*" The child pulled the door shut behind her.

Sarah finished the dishes, straightened up the living room, and sat down at the kitchen table with paper and pen. She had written a brief letter to her mother to say that she would not be returning to Lancaster Country, but she had also promised a much longer letter with details about her adventure, the man with amnesia and his return to the Amish faith.

A late afternoon haze was bending low over the yard, signaling the coming sunset, when she tucked the folded letter into her apron pocket and stepped to the window to look for Lyddie to return. But instead, the Amish taxi pulled into her lane. With a lightness in her step, she retrieved her cape and pulled it on as she stepped outside to see who it could be.

Jed sat in the front seat. He stepped out of the vehicle, his large smile warming her from the winter cold. He retrieved a couple of bags from the back seat and moved quickly to her as the Amish taxi pulled away.

"You are done so soon? I thought it would be a few more days."

He grasped her hand in his, shaking his head *no*. "I testified at the trial, and guilty verdicts were returned for both early this afternoon. So, I rushed out of the courthouse, grabbed my few things, and the Amish taxi picked me up and drove me directly here. I didn't want to wait any longer."

"But you will have to return, *jah*?"

"Yes, but just to finish up a couple of things." He meandered toward the house, still holding her hand. "I just didn't want to wait any longer to leave that nine to five behind and slow down. Live simply."

"And eat pie?" She tossed a teasing smile

at him, the pressure of her hand in his making her heart thump and bump.

"*Jah*, always pie." He returned the smile. "I know there will be hard work. But it'll be work with the satisfaction of a job well done, work with the strength of my hands as well as my mind."

"And your medical tests? You have results?"

"Yes. Everything came back clear. I won't have any lasting damage. I saw my parents, and, although they don't understand my return to the Amish, they don't disapprove either." The smile grew wider across his handsome face. "It feels good to remember again. To remember everything."

"That is *gut*. I saw your *grossmammi* yesterday, *Mammi* Mary. She has your room ready."

"Yes, she wrote to me that she was eager to make up for lost time. I think she's going to keep me up nights talking and reminiscing. And I meet with the bishop tomorrow about being baptized into the church. Then," he turned to her and drew her into his arms, gently touching his lips to hers, "we have something else to decide."

"*Jah?*"

The sun broke free of the clouds just as

it hit the horizon. The rays of light shone in pink and purple across the snow and ice, and a thousand crystals sparkled in the sunset.

"A wedding date."

Sarah gasped as Jed put his fingers to her lips.

"I love you, Sarah Burkholder. It would be an honor if you would be my wife and if Lyddie would be my daughter. Will you marry me?"

Sarah's heart thumped a wild beat. Here was the moment she had been wondering over and praying about for the last two weeks. But before she could answer, Lyddie burst from the woods, pulling her sled, Snowball bounding beside her. She ran to Jed, and he picked her up, gathering Sarah back into his embrace, as well. "Jed, you are here to stay?"

"Well, that's up to your mother." He looked to her, pleading in his eyes, his eyebrows raised with the unanswered question.

A lump formed in her throat. How did she deserve all this happiness? All this answered prayer? She swallowed hard. "*Jah*, I will."

Jed squeezed them both tight and answered Lyddie's question without removing his gaze from Sarah. "*Jah*, little one, I'm here to stay."

"Will you become my *daed*?"

Sarah's heart danced within her. A tear squeezed out to expose her joy.

"As soon as the bishop will allow it, *liebchen*."

She leaned to give Lyddie a kiss on the cheek, followed by a kiss on Jed's cheek, and the letter to her mother that she had tucked into her pocket pressed against her. It wasn't the letter she had written a couple of weeks ago. That letter had burned in the barn fire, a fitting end to the intentions she had expressed in it. Even then, she had known she didn't want to continue, especially not in Indiana, without Jed.

Now, she would write a new letter. A letter that explained it all. Jed was hers, and she was Jed's. Her home was here, with him, in Indiana. Sarah's lips found his as Lyddie hugged them both around the legs, completeness and wholeness settling over her like a warm Amish quilt.

* * * * *

Dear Reader,

Thank you for reading my first Amish suspense. It was a thrill to write, and I pray it was a thrill to read.

John had quite a struggle with his memory loss and his faith. Even though there wasn't much he could do to jog his memory, his faith just needed a little encouragement. Isn't that the way it is sometimes? I know there have been moments in my life in which I knew what to do, but I appreciated encouragement. The Lord is there, through His Word and through prayer.

As she ran for her life, Sarah struggled with the constant reminder of the fleeting nature of existence. I admire her determination to take life a day at a time and trust *Gott* in all things. She learned to number her days as God revealed to her that He did not want her to be miserable after the death of her husband. God has good things in store for us, and she determined to rejoice in each day.

I would be honored to hear from you. You can visit my website at *www.MeghanCarver.com*, where you can sign up for my author newsletter, or email me at MeghanCCarver@gmail.com. If you're on Facebook, I'd like to be your friend at Facebook.com/Meghan-Carver. If you wish to write on good old-fashioned stationery, you can send it to me c/o Love Inspired Books, 195 Broadway, 24th Floor, New York, NY 10007.

Many blessings to you,
Meghan Carver

Get 4 FREE REWARDS!

We'll send you 2 FREE Books plus 2 FREE Mystery Gifts.

Love Inspired® books feature contemporary inspirational romances with Christian characters facing the challenges of life and love.

FREE
Value Over
$20

YES! Please send me 2 FREE Love Inspired® Romance novels and my 2 FREE mystery gifts (gifts are worth about $10 retail). After receiving them, if I don't wish to receive any more books, I can return the shipping statement marked "cancel." If I don't cancel, I will receive 6 brand-new novels every month and be billed just $5.24 for the regular-print edition or $5.74 each for the larger-print edition in the U.S., or $5.74 each for the regular-print edition or $6.24 each for the larger-print edition in Canada. That's a savings of at least 13% off the cover price. It's quite a bargain! Shipping and handling is just 50¢ per book in the U.S. and 75¢ per book in Canada*. I understand that accepting the 2 free books and gifts places me under no obligation to buy anything. I can always return a shipment and cancel at any time. The free books and gifts are mine to keep no matter what I decide.

Choose one: ☐ **Love Inspired® Romance**
Regular-Print
(105/305 IDN GMY4)

☐ **Love Inspired® Romance**
Larger-Print
(122/322 IDN GMY4)

Name (please print)

Address   Apt. #

City   State/Province   Zip/Postal Code

Mail to the **Reader Service:**
IN U.S.A.: P.O. Box 1341, Buffalo, NY 14240-8531
IN CANADA: P.O. Box 603, Fort Erie, Ontario L2A 5X3

Want to try two free books from another series! Call 1-800-873-8635 or visit www.ReaderService.com.

---

*Terms and prices subject to change without notice. Prices do not include applicable taxes. Sales tax applicable in N.Y. Canadian residents will be charged applicable taxes. Offer not valid in Quebec. This offer is limited to one order per household. Books received may not be as shown. Not valid for current subscribers to Love Inspired Romance books. All orders subject to approval. Credit or debit balances in a customer's account(s) may be offset by any other outstanding balance owed by or to the customer. Please allow 4 to 6 weeks for delivery. Offer available while quantities last.

Your Privacy—The Reader Service is committed to protecting your privacy. Our Privacy Policy is available online at www.ReaderService.com or upon request from the Reader Service. We make a portion of our mailing list available to reputable third parties that offer products we believe may interest you. If you prefer that we not exchange your name with third parties, or if you wish to clarify or modify your communication preferences, please visit us at www.ReaderService.com/consumerschoice or write to us at Reader Service Preference Service, P.O. Box 9062, Buffalo, NY 14240-9062. Include your complete name and address.

LI18

Get 4 FREE REWARDS!

We'll send you 2 FREE Books
plus 2 FREE Mystery Gifts.

Harlequin® Heartwarming™ Larger-Print books feature traditional values of home, family, community and most of all—love.

FREE
Value Over
$20

HOME on the RANCH

YES! Please send me the **Home on the Ranch Collection** in Larger Print. This collection begins with 3 FREE books and 2 FREE gifts in the first shipment. Along with my 3 free books, I'll also get the next 4 books from the Home on the Ranch Collection, in LARGER PRINT, which I may either return and owe nothing, or keep for the low price of $5.24 U.S./ $5.89 CDN each plus $2.99 for shipping and handling per shipment*. If I decide to continue, about once a month for 8 months I will get 6 or 7 more books, but will only need to pay for 4. That means 2 or 3 books in every shipment will be FREE! If I decide to keep the entire collection, I'll have paid for only 32 books because 19 books are FREE! I understand that accepting the 3 free books and gifts places me under no obligation to buy anything. I can always return a shipment and cancel at any time. My free books and gifts are mine to keep no matter what I decide.

268 HCN 3760 468 HCN 3760

Name _____ (PLEASE PRINT)

Address _____ Apt. #

City _____ State/Prov. _____ Zip/Postal Code

Signature (if under 18, a parent or guardian must sign)

Mail to the **Reader Service:**

IN U.S.A.: P.O. Box 1341, Buffalo, New York 14240-8531
IN CANADA: P.O. Box 603, Fort Erie, Ontario L2A 5X3

* Terms and prices subject to change without notice. Prices do not include applicable taxes. Sales tax applicable in NY. Canadian residents will be charged applicable taxes. This offer is limited to one order per household. All orders subject to approval. Credit or debit balances in a customer's account(s) may be offset by any other outstanding balance owed by or to the customer. Please allow 3 to 4 weeks for delivery. Offer available while quantities last. Offer not available to Quebec residents.

Your Privacy—The Reader Service is committed to protecting your privacy. Our Privacy Policy is available online at www.ReaderService.com or upon request from the Reader Service.

We make a portion of our mailing list available to reputable third parties that offer products we believe may interest you. If you prefer that we not exchange your name with third parties, or if you wish to clarify or modify your communication preferences, please visit us at www.ReaderService.com/consumerschoice or write to us at Reader Service Preference Service, P.O. Box 9062, Buffalo, NY. 14240-9062. Include your complete name and address.